Laurie Saw The Man's Legs First—Long And Lean, Encased In Faded Blue Jeans.

As his feet hit the ground, her gaze traveled upward to take in the slim hips, flat stomach and broad shoulders, challenging the seams of a white Western-cut shirt. He was looking down as he hit the ground, and his face and hair were obscured by a pearl gray Stetson. So it was only when he focused directly on her that she saw the lean, weather-whipped face, the sensual lips, the steel blue eyes—features once as familiar to her as her own reflection in the mirror.

"Oh...my...God," she murmured. Then every cubic inch of oxygen deserted her lungs.

"Hi, Laurie."

"'Hi, Laurie'?" she repeated. "Is that all you have to say? You're supposed to be dead!"

Dear Reader,

It's hard to believe that this is the grand finale of CELEBRATION 1000! But all good things must come to an end. Not that there aren't more wonderful things in store for you next month, too....

But as for June, first we have an absolutely sizzling MAN OF THE MONTH from Ann Major called *The Accidental Bodyguard*.

Are you a fan of HAWK'S WAY? If so, don't miss the latest "Hawk's" story, *The Temporary Groom* by Joan Johnston. Check out the family tree on page six and see if you recognize all the members of the Whitelaw family.

And with *The Cowboy and the Cradle* Cait London has begun a fabulous new western series—THE TALLCHIEFS. (P.S. The next Tallchief is all set for September!)

Many of you have written to say how much you love Elizabeth Bevarly's books. Her latest, *Father of the Brood*, book #2 in the FROM HERE TO PATERNITY series, simply shouldn't be missed.

This month is completed with Karen Leabo's *The Prodigal Groom*, the latest in our WEDDING NIGHT series, and don't miss a wonderful star of tomorrow— DEBUT AUTHOR Eileen Wilks, who's written *The Loner and the Lady*.

As for next month...we have a not-to-be-missed MAN OF THE MONTH by Anne McAllister, and Dixie Browning launches DADDY KNOWS LAST, a new Silhouette continuity series beginning in Desire.

Lucia Macro

Senior Editor

Please address questions and book requests to:
Silhouette Reader Service
U.S.: 3010 Walden Ave., P.O. Box 1325, Buffalo, NY 14269
Canadian: P.O. Box 609, Fort Erie, Ont. L2A 5X3

KAREN LEABO
THE PRODIGAL GROOM

SILHOUETTE *Desire*®
Published by Silhouette Books
America's Publisher of Contemporary Romance

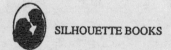 SILHOUETTE BOOKS

ISBN 0-373-76007-8

THE PRODIGAL GROOM

Books by Karen Leabo

Silhouette Desire

Close Quarters #629
Lindy and the Law #676
Unearthly Delights #704
The Cop #767
Ben #794
Feathers and Lace #824
Twilight Man #838
Megan's Miracle #880
Beach Baby #923
Man Overboard #946
The Prodigal Groom #1007

Silhouette Romance

Roses Have Thorns #648
Ten Days in Paradise #692
Domestic Bliss #707
Full Bloom #731
Smart Stuff #764
Runaway Bride #797
The Housewarming #848
A Changed Man #886

Silhouette Intimate Moments

Into Thin Air #619

KAREN LEABO

credits her fourth-grade teacher with initially sparking her interest in creative writing. She was determined at an early age to have her work published. When she was in the eighth grade she wrote a children's book and convinced her school yearbook publisher to put it in print.

Karen was born and raised in Dallas. She has worked as a magazine art director, a free-lance writer and a textbook editor, but now she keeps herself busy full-time writing about romance.

Dear Reader,

They don't put red covers on Silhouette Desires for nothing! The first time I read one—had to be a dozen years ago—I was pleasantly surprised to find that the hero and heroine didn't close the bedroom door. Beautifully detailed love scenes were an essential part of the story, providing something I'd felt was missing from those "tamer" romances.

Desires quickly became my favorite reads, not only because I liked the love scenes, but because I could relate to the modern, fast-paced tone of these books. The blend of fantasy and real-life people appealed to me as a reader. I could cast myself as the heroine and feel right at home.

When I decided to try my hand at writing romance, Silhouette Desire was where I wanted to be. I was proud as a new mother when my first Desire, *Close Quarters*, was published in 1991, and even happier that Desire has been my publishing "home" for many years now.

Needless to say, it's a great honor to have one of my books chosen for CELEBRATION 1000. *The Prodigal Groom* is a special book for me because I took all of those reader favorites—a bride, a ranch, a secret baby and a cowboy/cop—and put them all into one story!

I hope you'll enjoy all of the Celebration 1000 Desires, and I hope you'll see my name on one of those bright red covers when it comes time for CELEBRATION 2000!

Karen Leabo

Prologue

The room was abominably hot, and the smell of roses was overpowering. Laurie Branson tugged at the choking neckline of her antique satin dress, readjusted her itchy headpiece, then glanced at her watch yet again.

"He's a half hour late," Laurie's sister, Katie, said needlessly. Everyone in the room was excruciatingly aware of the time, and of the groom's continued absence. Hell, the way gossip flew in Winnefred, Texas, probably everyone in town knew by now that Jake Mercer was late for his own wedding.

Five more minutes crawled by.

"Well, we might as well face it," said Throckmore Branson, Laurie's father. "He's not coming. Once again, Jake Mercer has made his work more important than you, Laurie. Only this time he's blown a twenty-thousand-dollar wedding. I hope you're satisfied, because this is the only wedding you'll get!"

"Throck..." Laurie's mother, Louise, laid a gentling hand on her husband's arm.

"No, let me finish," he said. "This has needed to be said for a long time. Mercer is a dedicated lawman, I'll give him that, but he's more married to his career than he'll ever be to any woman. He's been inconsiderate toward you from the start, Laurie, always putting himself before you, always thinking his needs were more important than yours.

"I warned you he was too old for you, too set in his ways to take on a young wife, possibly children, as well. He's simply not the type of man to put his family first. Now, can you see I was right? Any man who would run off to chase down some scumbag drug dealer instead of marrying the girl he supposedly loves—"

"Yes, I get the point, Daddy," Laurie interrupted. "He's undependable and a rotten prospect for a husband." And she loved him with every cell in her body. Hadn't she told him that last night, for the hundredth time? And hadn't he shown her, in his own feverish way, how much he cared?

Old-fashioned as it was, she had wanted to wait until their wedding night to physically consummate that love. The emotion that raged between them had felt so pure to her, so sacred, that it hadn't seemed right to bring premarital sex into the picture. She'd wanted their first time together to be sanctioned by the church and God, so there would be no guilt or shame or fear of pregnancy to mar the experience, and Jake had agreed.

Last night, however, all their good intentions had gone straight out the window. Feeling a little giddy from the wine at the rehearsal dinner, and so full of love for the man she was about to marry that she thought she would burst, Laurie had succumbed to the fulminating desires that had plagued her for months. Jake had been the cautious one, insisting that she be very sure in her own mind they were doing the right thing.

She'd been positive. After all, she was so committed to him that she already felt married. What difference did a few hours make?

Their lovemaking had been everything she'd fantasized about and more. Her face grew warm even thinking about it. Jake had demonstrated his love for her in a dozen different ways. And she'd believed in it. How could she ever regret something so beautiful?

She still believed in that love. Jake had promised he would be here, despite the fact that his Special Operations Group had been called in early this morning to apprehend fugitive drug lord Juan LaBarba.

Jake had explained over the phone that the operation would be swift and clean. He and the other men would be in and out before LaBarba and his gang even knew anyone was within spitting distance. And he would make it to the church with plenty of time to spare.

But if that had been the case, where was Jake?

"Something must have gone wrong," she murmured.

"I'll tell you what went wrong," her father said. "Cold feet."

Laurie stood, her bouquet of white roses falling unheeded to the wine-colored carpet. "I hope you're right. I hope that's all it is—cold feet. But did it ever occur to you—to any of you," she added, taking in her mother and the four bridesmaids, who had remained silently disapproving throughout this ordeal, "that something might have happened to Jake? That he might be injured? The LaBarbas have guns, and they're not afraid to use them."

"I'm sure it's nothing like that," Louise said. "Let's not jump to any conclusions until we hear from Jake. Meanwhile..." She looked at her watch. "Perhaps we should make a decision?"

"Fine. I'll go tell everyone the wedding's off," Laurie said curtly. She ought to be crying or something, she thought. But she couldn't. She was a tensed-up ball of nerves, and she wouldn't be able to release anything until she found out what had happened.

She straightened her spine and walked toward the door, curiously unconcerned about the embarrassment of letting the whole town know she'd been jilted. But the door opened before she could reach it and her older brother, Danny, entered, his face as white as the rosebud he wore in his lapel.

"Laurie, I think you'd better sit down," he said.

She knew what was coming even before he related the facts in an emotionless voice. The bust had gone bad. LaBarba's brother, Ernesto, had been shot and captured, but Juan had gotten away. And somehow, in the process, Jake had been killed.

Again, Laurie thought she should cry or scream or faint or something. But a cold lump of numbness grew inside her until it encompassed her whole being. "Where is he?" she asked in a voice that sounded like a worn-out tape recording.

"No one knows," Danny said. "The LaBarbas took his...his body when they fled."

Laurie was vaguely aware of her mother's arm around her shoulders, her father's gruff words of condolence, the pain in her brother's eyes. She wanted to respond, but she couldn't. Her limbs were like lead, and her mouth wouldn't cooperate when she tried to speak.

KAREN LEABO 11

She could have forgiven Jake for missing their wedding. She could have forgiven him for his dedication in pursuing an evil man like Juan LaBarba. But she would never, ever, forgive him for dying.

One

It was time, Jake Mercer thought. He stopped his pickup truck at the end of a long, red-dirt driveway and contemplated the sign that marked the entrance to Birkett's Folly. Yeah, Charlie Birkett had done all right for himself with this place. Jake had gotten to where he could identify Birkett horseflesh at every rodeo he went to in these parts.

But all was not as prosperous at the Folly as appearances would indicate. If he looked close, Jake could see that the fence needed painting. And there weren't quite as many sleek quarter horses grazing in the pasture as there used to be.

But even before he'd seen those clues, Jake had known something wasn't right here. He'd sensed deep trouble the moment he'd seen the classified ad placed by Laurie Branson Birkett:

WANTED: Manager for established quarter-horse ranch. Must have experience in financial management and know the specifics of equine breeding. Living quarters provided. Salary negotiable. Apply in person, Birkett's Folly, Winnefred, Texas, or call . . .

Jake had heard through the grapevine that Laurie was having a hard time of it after her husband's fatal stroke, but he'd assumed that meant she was grieving. He'd never dreamed that Charlie Birkett hadn't adequately provided for his wife in the event of his death. Surely he'd made provisions for someone to take over management of the Folly.

Then again, knowing Laurie, she'd probably insisted she could manage things herself—never mind that when she'd married Charlie, a scant two months after Jake's disappearance, she hadn't known one end of a horse from the other. In fact, as he recalled, she'd been scared of horses.

Well, whatever, she obviously was in need of a manager now. Jake had grown up on a cattle ranch. Although his family hadn't bred quarter horses, they'd bought and sold a fair number of them over the years— many from the Birketts—and Jake could recognize championship qualities when he saw them. In fact, he currently owned a Birkett horse, a stallion he'd picked up for a song because the horse had been lame.

He could help Laurie. And if she was in financial straits, as it appeared she was, he could help her for a lot less salary than any other applicants who might wander to her door.

Maybe it was a crazy thing to do, showing up in her life after four years. But for most of that time he'd been

keeping track of her, reading about her in the Winnefred weekly newspaper and savoring bits of information reluctantly dragged from her brother, Danny. Those
scraps weren't enough anymore.

He had to see her. He wanted to help her, and, hell, he
owed her that much at least.

Yeah, it was time. He put his truck into gear and
turned into the driveway.

Laurie stretched on tiptoes to fasten the corner of the
last damp sheet to the clothesline. There, that task was
done. But it had taken thirty minutes out of her day,
thirty minutes she hadn't planned on.

Honestly, if it wasn't one thing it was another. This
morning the clothes dryer had quit abruptly. Replacing
it was out of the question, given the state of her house-
hold budget. At least the spring weather was pleasant.
She wondered how people without clothes dryers took
care of their laundry in the middle of winter.

"All done?" asked three-year-old Wendy. She was
sitting in the empty laundry basket with two striped kittens in her lap, making Laurie wish she could run and get
her camera. But there just wasn't time.

"All done," she answered, plucking up one of the
kittens and cuddling it under her chin. They were supposed to be barn cats, not house pets, kept solely to take
care of the rodent population, but Wendy had relentlessly tamed them. "Want to help me weed the garden?"

"Mmm, okay, but my tummy's growling."

Laurie looked at her watch. Darn, it was almost noon.
How had the morning gotten away from her? She still
had to call the vet and find out if there was any news
about Flash's lab tests. And she had to check the an-

swering machine to see if anyone had responded to the
ad she'd placed in the Tyler paper.

She half hoped no one would apply for the job. Although she was perilously close to financial disaster, she
hated the thought of some stranger moving in and running things.

After Charlie's unexpected death, she had arrogantly
assumed she could take over running the Folly. After all,
she was a college graduate with retail management experience, and she'd lived and helped out at the Folly for
four years. There was also Maurice, who'd been working the Folly for more than a decade, to help her.

But she'd quickly discovered that managing a ranch
wasn't quite like managing a gift shop, which was what
she'd done until she'd married Charlie. She'd had no
clue as to which mares should be bred to which stud, or
how much to pay for the service of this stud or that one,
or when and how much to sell the horses for. While
Charlie had kept meticulous records, Laurie had found
them less intelligible than a physics textbook. There just
didn't seem to be a pattern.

And Maurice, for all his expertise in handling the
horses, knew very little about the money end of things.

Still, Laurie had persevered, plunging into one fool-
ish choice after another. Charlie's illness, brief though
it was, had depleted their cash, and everything she'd
done had made the situation worse. She'd waited far too
long to admit she needed help. Now, she was afraid it
was too late. If she lost the Folly, she didn't know what
she would do. Oh, they could survive, but the ranch was
her daughter's legacy.

"Maurice!" Wendy cried out as the Folly's truck
rumbled down the driveway. She scrambled out of the

basket and ran to the edge of the yard, ready to greet Maurice Bryson, the Folly's only remaining employee.

"Hello, Sunshine," Maurice said as he unfolded his long frame and climbed out of the truck. "And good morning to you, Miz Laurie. I brought your mail."

"Thanks, Maurice. I'm afraid to ask, but what was wrong with the truck, and how much did it cost to fix it?"

"Water pump. Not too much." He handed a receipt to Laurie along with the stack of letters. She winced. Could have been worse, she supposed.

Wendy tugged at Maurice's pants leg. "Are you my daddy?" she asked earnestly.

Maurice let loose with a roar of laughter, then picked Wendy up and swung her into the air. "No, Sunshine, I'm afraid my skin's just a tad too dark for me to be your daddy. But I can be your honorary uncle, how 'bout that?" He set her down and patted her on the head.

"Wendy!" Laurie was mortified. "I'm sorry, Maurice. Ever since she figured out that all the other kids at her preschool have daddies, she's been obsessed with the concept. Wendy," she said sternly, "I've told you before, your daddy's in heaven. I've shown you his picture."

"But that's not fair," she said, stamping her little foot. "When's he coming back?"

"Sweetheart, he can't come back. He's with the angels."

"Then I want a new daddy. Cindy has two. Why can't I have one of hers?"

Ah, the logic of three-year-olds. Thankfully, Laurie was saved from answering by the timely arrival of a visitor. A shiny blue pickup truck was barreling down the long driveway, raising a cloud of red dust. Laurie's immediate reaction was to covet the truck, which was so much newer and nicer than hers, but she chastised herself. She had to stop wishing for the impossible and play the hand she'd been dealt.

Hadn't that always been the way of it?

"Mommy, I have to go tinkle," Wendy said, forgetting her daddy obsession for the moment.

"Run inside if you have to use the bathroom," Laurie said. She abhorred the term *tinkle,* another lovely concept her daughter had picked up at her weekly preschool. "I'll be in in a minute to start lunch."

"Okay." Wendy picked up one of the kittens, draped the compliant beast over her shoulder and headed for the front porch of the sprawling white frame house, which had been in the Birkett family for four generations.

Maurice cast a curious glance over his shoulder as the truck drew closer. "I'll set that mail on the front porch for you."

Laurie handed him the packet of letters and catalogs, which she'd scarcely glanced at. "Thanks. Don't stray too far. I have no idea who's driving that truck." Winnefred was a friendly little town, certainly no hotbed of crime, but as a woman living alone in the country, Laurie was aware of how vulnerable she was.

The blue truck pulled up behind the Folly's truck and stopped. Someone applying for the job, perhaps? His vehicle certainly qualified, she thought guiltily, tucking a stray lock of hair behind her ear. She wished she'd put on a nicer blouse this morning, instead of one that was faded and frayed at the cuffs.

The truck's door opened, and Laurie saw the man's alligator boots first, then his legs—long and lean, encased in faded blue jeans. As his feet hit the ground, her gaze traveled upward to take in the slim hips, flat stomach and broad shoulders challenging the seams of a white western-cut shirt. He was looking down as he hit the ground, and his face and hair were obscured by a pearl gray Stetson. So it was only when he focused directly on her that she saw the lean, weather-whipped face, the sensual lips, the steel blue eyes, features once as familiar to her as her own reflection in the mirror.

"Oh...my...God," she murmured. Then every cubic inch of oxygen deserted her lungs.

"Hi, Laurie." He removed his hat, revealing his black hair, long and wavy on top but shorter on the sides than she remembered. It gleamed in the sun like a crow's wing.

"Hi, Laurie?" she repeated, the words choked. "Is that all you have to say? You're supposed to be dead!" With that the world imploded to a pinpoint of light and the ground tipped sideways. The last thing she remembered was a strong pair of arms breaking her fall.

Jake lowered her gently to the grass. "Laurie? Laurie, honey, wake up," he said, patting her cheek.

Ah, hell, he supposed he shouldn't have taken her by surprise like this. But she'd never been the fainting type.

"Here, now, what's going on?" A tall, wiry black man came barreling around the side of the house with a shotgun pointed at Jake's heart.

Jake jumped away from Laurie. "Whoa, there. Easy with that gun. She just fainted, that's all."

Maurice lowered the gun and stared with shooter-marble eyes. "Jake? Jake Mercer? But you can't be him, 'cause he's dead."

"It's me, all right, Maurice," Jake said, recalling the ranch hand's name.

Laurie stirred and moaned. Jake immediately hunkered down and touched her face, smoothing a strand of sun-bright hair off her cheek.

"Laurie? You okay?"

Her bleary eyes tried their best to focus on him. She blinked several times. "Oh, God, it is you, Jake. Are you a ghost? Or am I dead, too?"

He smiled gently. "No, you're very much alive." And her nearness affected him in ways he'd forgotten. His heart pounded and his gut tightened, and he wanted nothing more than to draw her into his arms and cling to her vitality. Her memory had kept him alive during those long, hard months of captivity. Now he was finding out that his memory hadn't done her justice.

"You cut your hair," he said.

Laurie pushed herself into a sitting position. "I hardly think that's relevant! What are you doing here? How did you...? What on earth...? I don't know whether to be happy to see you or furious!"

He offered his hand. "Let's go inside where it's cool and get you something to drink, and I promise I'll answer every one of your questions."

She allowed him to help her to her feet, though she released his hand the moment she was steady. "All right," she said uncertainly, glancing nervously toward the front porch. "But I've got to get lunch on the table, so we'll have to talk in the kitchen."

Jake's gaze followed hers, and he immediately saw what was troubling her. A blond-haired toddler in a gingham dress stood on the porch, clinging to a rocking chair, her angelic little face filled with suspicion as she stared at Jake.

"Oh, Lord, Laurie, she's beautiful." He barely breathed the words. "Looks just like you did at that age."

Laurie's gaze darted back and forth between Jake and the child. "She's—that's Wendy, my daughter."

"Mommy? Are you sick?"

Laurie went to her. "No, sweetheart, I'm just fine. Are you ready for some lunch?"

The little girl nodded distractedly, still staring at Jake.

Laurie took Wendy's hand and entered the house. Maurice followed, and neither of them made a point of inviting Jake in. He went in, anyway. This wasn't exactly the joyful reunion he'd expected.

"Laurie," Maurice said, "you want I should take Wendy into town for a hamburger? Then you and Jake can talk."

"Oh, that'd be terrific," she answered, silently thanking heaven that Maurice was so perceptive. She grabbed her purse, which was hanging on a hook by the door, and pulled out her wallet. "Drat, I haven't got more than a couple of dollars in here."

"I'll get it," Jake said, quickly pulling a twenty from his own wallet. Maurice took it with a nod.

"Thank you," Laurie said grudgingly. "Wendy, Maurice will take you to Dairy Queen, okay?"

The child nodded, but she was still studying Jake. Abruptly she ran toward him and grabbed on to his leg. "Daddy!" she shrieked.

Obviously horrified, Laurie pulled her daughter away. "No, Wendy," she said sharply. "Remember what we talked about? Your daddy's in heaven."

Wendy folded her arms and firmed her mouth up in a mutinous expression, clearly not buying her mother's explanation. Jake would have laughed if the situation hadn't been so poignant.

"C'mon, Sunshine," Maurice interjected. "Let's go get some hamburgers. And I bet Mommy'll let us get some ice cream afterward. What do you say?"

Wendy grabbed on to the hand Maurice offered and allowed herself to be led away, but even the promise of ice cream hadn't completely distracted her from her fixation on Jake. She looked over her shoulder, continuing to stare at him with solemn blue eyes until the front door closed, blocking him from view.

"I bet she's a handful," Jake said, feeling suddenly achy around his heart. He and Laurie had intended to have children, lots of them.

"She is," Laurie said, her voice still a bit weak. "Sweet and cuddly one minute and stubborn as a mule the next. I'm sorry...I don't know what to say. She never knew her...Charlie. Lately she's become obsessed with finding her daddy." Laurie waited, holding her breath, expecting some acknowledgment from Jake that he would soon rectify the situation.

"It's okay," he said with a shrug, dismissing the incident far more casually than she would have believed possible. "Hey, you look like you're about to keel over again. Let's get you some water." With a hand at the small of her back, he guided her to the kitchen. He remembered where it was from visits to Birkett's Folly as a child. His father and old Will Birkett had been good friends.

The absurdity of this situation made Laurie want to laugh. Jake Mercer was alive? How often had she dreamed that it was all a big misunderstanding, that the Marshals Service had made a mistake? Apparently those farfetched dreams were coming true.

Again she stifled an almost hysterical laugh. On the heels of her elation, however, came anger. How dare Jake come back from the dead? How dare he abandon her, abandon their child, then blithely waltz back into her life unannounced?

Oh, Lord, she was confused, still woozy and weak, and if she didn't get herself something to eat or drink she was going to faint again. So she said nothing as Jake took a glass from the cabinet and filled it with cold water from the refrigerator.

He handed it to her. She took it, carefully avoiding touching him, and took several long swallows.

"Sit down," Jake said.

She would have remained standing just to prove he couldn't tell her what to do, but her legs wouldn't cooperate. She sank into the chair he held out for her.

He sat down across from her, with the old enamel kitchen table between them. Her dizziness abated and her wits began to return. Now maybe she was in some kind of shape to listen to Jake's explanations.

Surely he didn't expect to take up with her where he'd left off.

"So, talk," she said. "Where have you been for the past four years? Now, let's see, maybe I can guess. Juan LaBarba swore a vendetta against you, so the blessed U.S. Marshals Service decided to hide you for a while, and they told us you died so we wouldn't come looking for you. Am I close?"

"Nowhere near." He rested his hands on the edge of the table and rocked back and forth a couple of times. "Laurie, do you actually believe I'd leave you standing at the altar because of some stupid vendetta?"

Properly chastised for jumping to conclusions, she shook her head. "I'm sorry. Tell me what really happened."

"I was shot and left for dead," he said quietly. "I got caught in the same flurry of gunfire that killed Ernesto LaBarba, Juan's brother. The LaBarbas dragged me inside the building where they were holed up, thinking to trade me for Ernesto. But when they found out Ernesto had died, they decided to keep me as a bargaining chip. They fled to Costa Rica and took me with them."

"Did you try to escape?" Laurie asked, trying to fathom the horror he must have experienced. It sounded so unreal, like a bad movie.

"I wasn't in any shape to escape. Juan's wife, Carmen, patched me up pretty good, but I still got some kind of infection that lasted for months. I don't remember a whole lot about that time."

Laurie winced. What he must have gone through! She wanted to touch him, to offer him comfort, but the look in his eyes told her he hadn't come to her for pity. "So did they use you as a bargaining chip, like they intended?" she asked.

"Apparently they tried, but by then the government was denying all knowledge of me. As far as they were concerned, I was dead—and they didn't want anyone to contradict them."

"But..." she started to object, then paused when Jake pulled a bit of metal out of his jeans pocket and laid it on the table.

"That's the bullet Carmen found in me. It was from one of our guns, not the Uzis LaBarba's gang was using."

"My God, you were shot by one of your own men," she said, barely breathing the words. "It wasn't intentional, was it?"

He shook his head. "I'm sure it was an accident. All hell was breaking loose. Nerves were pulled to the breaking point."

"Still, I can see why they wouldn't want you spreading it around that you were the victim of 'friendly fire.'"

"Particularly since, in their official report, I was shot in the head, not the back." Bitterness twisted his mouth. "Apparently they weren't as sure that I was dead as they pretended, and they wanted to make damn certain no one else questioned it."

"So what did LaBarba do when he found out you weren't—" she paused, choosing just the right word "—valuable to them?"

"He would have killed me outright and left me for the buzzards, but Carmen intervened. I'm not sure exactly what she did, but LaBarba listened to her for some reason."

There was a certain kindness to Jake's expression when he talked about Carmen, and Laurie felt a pang of jealousy. Had he and Carmen...? Oh, surely Jake wouldn't get involved with another man's wife! She pushed the irrelevant thoughts aside.

"LaBarba might have had other plans for me. I don't know," Jake continued. "But I didn't wait around to find out. As soon as I was strong enough, I got the hell out of there. The first person I called when I got back to the States was Danny."

Danny. Her brother and Jake's best friend. It bothered her that Jake hadn't called her first. "When was this?"

"About..." He hesitated. "Shortly after Wendy was born."

Laurie was out of her chair. "You've been back for more than three years, and you waited until now to contact me? You let me think you were dead all this time? Danny knew, and he didn't tell me?" She was so angry and frustrated at the unfairness that she wanted to hit something. She settled for the tabletop, slapping it with the palm of her hand and almost upsetting her glass of water. "Why? Why didn't you come back to me?"

"Because, Laurie, you were married to another man."

Two

Laurie fell back into her chair with a thunk. Of course she'd been married. And Jake's sudden reappearance would have been awkward, to say the least. She wasn't sure that excused the fact that he'd continued to allow her to believe him dead, but there was some logic to his decision.

"I wanted to see you, believe me," Jake said, softening. "But Danny...convinced me otherwise. He said you'd finally gotten your life pulled together, and with the new baby and all...well, he just didn't think it would be fair for me to jump in and upset the applecart. Your brother can be very persuasive. I finally agreed with him," Jake concluded, rubbing his jaw.

You agreed to stay away from your own child? She almost said the words aloud, but something held her back. This whole situation was getting harder and harder to accept.

"Who else knows you're alive?" she asked, picturing the whole town whispering behind her back, pitying her in her ignorance.

"My folks, but that's about it. They retired in Tyler after they sold the ranch, and that's where I've been living, too, where I could keep an eye on them."

"How are they doing?" She was ashamed to admit she hadn't kept up with the elder Mercers. She had been to see them a few times after Jake's supposed death, which they'd taken hard. But after marrying Charlie—and as her pregnancy advanced—visiting the Mercers had seemed awkward, so she'd gradually let them slip away from her.

"They're holding their own," Jake replied with an unmistakable note of fondness. "I'd swear they aged ten years during the months I was gone, but they're doing better now. Anyway, I've made it a point to stay away from Winnefred. A couple of times I ran into people I knew, but I always managed to duck out of the way before they recognized me."

"Then why now?" Laurie asked, finally verbalizing the question she was most anxious about.

He took a deep breath and sighed. "It was time."

Laurie sighed, too, trying to adjust to this new reality. "You should have told me," she finally said. "I'm not saying it would have been easy, but I'm not a child. I was, and am, capable of making responsible decisions."

"Oh, you know how to make decisions, all right," he retorted, a sudden bitterness in his voice. "It didn't take you much time at all to decide to marry Charlie Birkett."

Laurie blinked a couple of times as she felt the blood draining from her face. Jake didn't know. He didn't know that she'd gotten pregnant as a result of the one and only time they'd made love. He didn't know that Wendy was his daughter. If he did, he would understand why she'd married Charlie so quickly.

How could Jake believe that she would marry anyone else if it hadn't been absolutely necessary? How could he think she would treat their love so trivially? A denial was on the tip of her tongue. But again, something held her back. If she blurted out the truth now, it might have far-reaching consequences, consequences she couldn't even imagine.

Wendy had been born seven months to the day after Laurie and Charlie had wed. Anyone with a lick of sense could count, and had figured out that the baby was Jake's, not Charlie's. In fact, Laurie was sure there had been a fair amount of gossip about it at the time. But no one had said anything to her or Charlie directly. And Charlie had been such a proud and doting father, that soon the whole town had embraced the idea that Wendy was really his.

Laurie didn't want that to change. Charlie had earned his place as Wendy's father. He had delighted in everything the child did, from kicking in the womb to flinging baby food on his good shirt. He had been as supportive of Laurie's situation as a man could be, and as devoted to Wendy as if the baby carried his genes. No one—not even Jake—was going to belittle Charlie's role in her family or dishonor his memory.

So she kept silent. She had to think carefully about this. She had to weigh Jake's right to know the truth with the possible repercussions.

"You're not even going to comment?" Jake asked, crossing his arms.

"No, I'm not," Laurie replied succinctly. She took a sip of her water to avoid looking into those steel blue eyes, afraid he would see that she was holding something back. Silence stretched uncomfortably between them. She could hear the old mantel clock ticking in the living room, and Maurice's mongrel dog barking at something.

Clearly frustrated, Jake rose abruptly and walked to the back door, then gazed out pensively at the mild spring day. "Steering clear of you seemed like the right decision at the time," he said. "Now, I'm not so sure. When I think about the years we lost, I have to wonder if I shouldn't have been more selfish about the whole thing. Maybe I should have barged in and tried to break up your marriage." He turned suddenly. "Would that have been better than my staying away?"

"You couldn't have broken up my marriage," she said. That was the one thing she was utterly sure of. Her marriage to Charlie may have lacked passion, but it had been strong in every other respect. She wouldn't have hurt that man for anything in the world, not even for Jake.

A muscle ticked in Jake's jaw. "Maybe that was why I stayed away. During those months in Costa Rica, thoughts of you were sometimes all that kept me alive. When I came back and found you were married . . ."

He must have been terribly hurt, she thought, though he would never put it in those terms.

"Maybe I was afraid you would turn me away," he said, "so I never even tried."

Her heart ached for him. She wanted to explain, but she couldn't, not yet. She had to give it some thought. And she couldn't think with Jake's overwhelming presence filling her kitchen and stealing her breath away every time she looked at him. Maturity had only sharpened his already awesome virility.

"Well, I'm glad you finally came forward," she said, the words woefully inadequate. "I'm glad you're not..."

"Not dead?"

That's what she'd been thinking, and it sounded awful. "Jake, I'm just too shocked to know what to say or how I feel. I think it would be better if you left." Before she said or did anything really stupid—like throwing her arms around him and absorbing his sheer aliveness.

He shook his head. "Not yet. I still have some business I want to discuss with you."

"What business?" she asked warily.

"I saw your ad in the Tyler paper. The one for the ranch manager," he added, as if she ran dozens of ads and needed clarification.

"And?"

"I'd like to apply for the position."

"Jake, don't be ridiculous!" she exploded. "Where would you get a fool notion like that?"

"Now, wait a minute, hear me out. It's not as crazy as it sounds."

"The hell it's not. You can't—"

"Laurie, let me explain."

She clamped her mouth shut. Apparently Jake was going to say his piece, and she wouldn't get him out of here until she let him.

"Now, then. I've heard some rumors that you're having problems here, and I can see just by looking around that they're true. Also, I know that you wouldn't be trying to hire a manager if you didn't need help. Just how bad is it?"

She considered lying. She didn't want to appear any more vulnerable to Jake than she already did. But she was afraid the sheer misery of her situation would shine through no matter what she said. "It's pretty bad," she confessed. "Our insurance wasn't adequate to cover the medical bills."

That was an understatement.

"I thought I could scrape by. I sold off some of the stock, but that cut into the Folly's income. Since then I've made some bad decisions." She shrugged helplessly.

Jake nodded, as if he'd suspected as much. "How do you intend to pay your new manager's salary?"

"Well...I was hoping to work something out. The position offers a nice little house, and I'd cook all the meals, like I already do for Maurice. Beyond that, I thought maybe some type of profit-sharing arrangement. The better job the manager does, the more money he makes."

Jake was shaking his head.

"It could work," Laurie said defensively.

"Have you had any qualified applicants?"

"Frankly, no, but the ad's only been running a few days."

"And do you honestly think a qualified applicant would work for you under those terms?"

"If he has vision," she answered. "If he's confident he can turn things around. The Folly once made bushels of money—and it will again. Anyway, if you think it's such a bad deal, why are you considering it?"

"Several reasons," he said, pacing the kitchen like a lawyer preparing to give a closing argument. "One, I know horses."

"You grew up with cattle," she said pointedly.

"But you can't run cattle without horses, and I've bought and sold more than a few. I might not be Charlie's equal when it comes to his knowledge about breeding, but it can't be that different from breeding cattle.''

She suspected it was a lot different, but since she knew nothing about cattle, she couldn't offer an intelligent argument. So she nodded, conceding the point.

"Two," Jake continued, ticking his points off on his fingers, "I don't need money, so it doesn't matter what you pay me."

"You don't need money?" she repeated, incredulous. She'd never met anyone who would admit that. Even rich folks who already had lots of money always claimed to need more.

"The government gave me a generous settlement for my, er, unscheduled vacation in Costa Rica," he said with a wry smile. "Actually, it was hush money. I was shot by my own man, the accounts of my death were falsified, and they made no effort to secure my release. They knew that, with a few well-chosen words in the right ears, I could have opened a huge can of worms. Not that I would have. I didn't need that kind of aggravation. But I didn't turn down the settlement."

"Okay, so you're set for life. That still doesn't explain why you would want to come here. Make no mistake, the manager's job won't be easy."

"Maybe I need a challenge," Jake said, reclaiming his chair across from her. "Maybe I need a change. I've been drifting aimlessly too long." He leaned across the table, until his face was uncomfortably close to hers. "But mostly, I want the job because I owe you something, Laurie. I promised to marry you, and I broke that promise. I put you through quite a bit of distress, I imagine."

"Distress? How about a living hell?" she retorted, suddenly angry again. Years ago she'd sworn she would never forgive him for leaving her alone, and that still held true.

"Must have been some living hell," he said, his fury matching hers. "Took you all of two months to find a replacement groom."

Perhaps he had a point, Laurie silently conceded. It must seem to Jake as if she'd gotten over her heartbreak pretty quickly. "Charlie helped me through it," she said simply. It was the truth.

"If I could go back and relive that day," Jake said quietly, "and do things differently, I would. Obviously I can't. But if I can help you out of this situation..."

"No," she said. "Not to soothe your conscience, not even if I really believed you could get me out of the mess I'm in. It could never work."

"You won't even consider it? On a temporary basis?"

"Absolutely not." The thought of seeing him every day, cooking dinner for him every night, brushed uncomfortably close to those girlish fantasies she'd once had before Jake's disappearance had shattered her life. Those dreams were wrapped securely in mental tissue paper and pushed far to the back of her mind—and they weren't getting out.

"You're being unreasonable," he said, rising slowly from his chair, towering over her intimidatingly. "If you don't get some help, and soon, you could lose the Folly."

She knew that, dammit. "I'll get some help. But not from you." Standing also, she stared at him, refusing to back down even an inch. That old electricity arced between them, and for one insane moment she thought he was looking not into her eyes, but at her mouth, and that he was thinking about kissing her.

The phone rang, cutting through the tension. Laurie turned abruptly to answer the old black wall phone. "Hello?"

Jake continued to watch her as he took a few steadying breaths. God, she was magnificent. She'd been a fiery, passionate girl when he'd last seen her. Now she was unmistakably a woman. Motherhood had added curves to her previously boyish figure. More importantly, the hardships she'd endured over the past four years had given her depth and maturity, and a certain air of mystery, too.

He had always been drawn to her, intrigued by her, and seriously attracted to her. During her absence from his life, that attraction hadn't diminished one iota. If anything, it was sharper, more intense, than ever.

He wished she hadn't cut her hair. He could still remember, as if it had been yesterday, the single night of passion they'd shared. He recalled the silky feel of her hair all around him, his fingers tangling in the long strands.

A change in her tone of voice brought Jake's attention back to the present. Who was she talking to?

"You're telling me there's no hope, that he's finished?" Laurie gripped the phone receiver so tightly her knuckles turned white. She nodded, biting her lower lip.

"Laurie, what's wrong?" Jake asked, moving around the table.

She turned away from him and faced the wall, but not before he could see that her eyes were unnaturally shiny. "All right. I'll have to think about it. I'll call in the morning." She hung up, chewing on her lip again.

"Laurie?" Unconsciously he reached out to touch her, but she shied away from him like a skittish filly.

"C'mon, Laurie, tell me what the problem is. Maybe I can help."

"It's...it's Flash in the Pan."

The Folly's highly sought-after stud. A two-time national quarter-horse champion more than a decade ago, Flash was the ranch's claim to fame and the source of a great deal of income. Mares were shipped from all over the country to be bred with the old stallion. Jake's own horse, Flash Lightning, had been sired by the original Flash.

"Is he sick?" Jake asked.

"In a manner of speaking. Last week, I decided to breed Flash with a new filly. She'd never been bred before, but she's the gentlest of creatures, and Flash is just a big old teddy bear. We—Maurice and I, that is—decided it would be okay just to turn them loose in the paddock and let nature take its course."

Jake winced. He had a feeling he knew what was coming next.

"Well, it wasn't okay. That ornery mare kicked him where it counts. My vet's been running tests on him, and she says Flash is permanently out of commission. Finished as a stud. She says I should have him g-gelded..." With that, the tears in her eyes spilled over.

"Oh, Laurie," Jake said, reaching for her again. This time she didn't stop him when he pulled her against his chest, but neither did she fully accept his comfort. She stood stiffly with his arms around her, sniffling miserably.

Laurie had never been weepy. Even as a little girl, when she'd fallen down or hurt herself, she'd struggled not to cry, especially if any boy, Jake included, was around to tease her. Jake could count on one hand the number of times he'd actually seen her give in to tears.

One of those times was when he'd asked her to marry him.

Jake rubbed her back with one hand and stroked her hair with the other. Her hair was as soft as he remembered, and it still smelled like green apples. He struggled to keep his hormones firmly under control. She was not exactly receptive to his attempt at comfort; he could just imagine what her reaction would be if she sensed his desire for her.

"It'll be okay," he crooned. "Flash is a tough guy, from what I hear. He'll come through this just fine."

But Jake knew she wasn't upset merely out of concern for the horse. Losing Flash's stud service could be a fatal blow to the struggling Folly. But not if Jake had anything to say about it. As it turned out, Flash's unhappy experience had given Jake the opening he needed, the ammunition that would convince Laurie he was the right man for the manager's job.

"Let go of me," Laurie said haughtily when she'd gotten the tears under control. "I can cry just fine without you."

Jake chuckled. "But why, when I have this big wide shoulder here to accommodate you?" Just the same, he released her, giving her shoulder one final pat.

She grabbed a paper napkin off the table and wiped her face. "I don't know why I'm getting so upset about this. Flash is an old horse. His macho days were numbered, anyway. His sperm count was getting lower every time I had him checked."

Jake stifled a chuckle. The old Laurie he'd known, his child bride, would never have talked so casually in front of him about sperm count. He supposed that living on a breeding farm for four years had toughened her up a bit.

"You have other studs, right?" he asked.

"None with Flash's lineage, or anything close to his reputation. People sought him out as much for his temperament as for his bloodline. He's so gentle."

That's what Jake wanted to hear. "So you've never kept one of Flash's sons or grandsons around as a backup?"

"Oh, we did, for a while. That was always Charlie's plan. But I sold him. Some rancher from Oklahoma offered me so much money for him I couldn't turn him down."

"What if I could get you the services of one of Flash's sons . . . for free?"

Laurie looked at him suspiciously, but curiously, too. "What are you talking about?"

"I happen to own a certain stallion named Flash Lightning—sired by Flash in the Pan, out of Heat Lightning."

"Heat Lightning? *The* Heat Lightning?"

"If you mean the grand champion barrel racer from Sulphur Springs, that's the one."

"How did you come by this horse?"

"His leg was shattered in a freak accident at a horse show I was at. They were talking about destroying him— his competition days were obviously over. But I couldn't stand to see such a beautiful animal destroyed, so I bought him and rehabilitated him. He's still lame, but I don't think that would interfere with his other capabilities."

Jake could almost see the wheels spinning in Laurie's mind. "How come I've never heard of this horse?"

"He didn't have much of a chance to earn a reputation for himself before his accident, but he showed a lot of potential. And I've never offered him up for stud because I didn't want to draw attention to myself.''

"But you'd let me use him . . . for free?''

"Provided you give me the manager's job. And, Laurie, Lightning is the spitting image of Flash in the Pan, right down to the white star on his chest. They could be twins.''

She opened her mouth to object, then clamped her mouth closed. Her expression was pensive. Jake could tell she was warring with herself, weighing the temptation of having Flash's son at her disposal with the inconvenience of having Jake himself underfoot.

"What if things didn't work out?'' Laurie asked. "What if you turn out to be a worse manager than me?''

"Give me five minutes' notice, and I'll leave.'' But he was pretty confident that wouldn't be the case. He would work his butt off to get this place back in shape.

If Laurie did end up kicking him off Birkett's Folly, it probably would be for a different reason. He'd had no intention of pursuing her, or engaging her in anything other than a friendly but professional relationship. He figured he'd given up the right to anything more the day he'd left her standing at the altar. But ever since he'd held her, filling his lungs with her scent, feeling her warmth and softness against him, he'd realized he would have a helluva time keeping his hands off her.

Laurie gave him a penetrating look. He stared back, waiting for her decision.

"When could you start?'' she asked in a less-than-confident voice.

Jake banked his elation. She was actually going to do it! "Is the house ready?''

She nodded. "It's clean, and the lights and water are turned on. There's some furniture, though not much, and nothing in the way of sheets and towels."

"I've got everything I need. I'll move in tonight, and I can start first thing in the morning."

Laurie nodded, not looking at all happy.

"You won't regret it, hon—Laurie, I promise." Damn, he'd almost called her "honey." It sure would be easy to fall into old habits, and that could get him in trouble. He shoved his Stetson on his head and got the heck out of there, before he could say or do anything else stupid.

Before she changed her mind.

Three

—

Laurie stared out the kitchen window, mesmerized, watching Jake walk around the barn taking notes, while Maurice pointed out leaks and storm damage. In his comfortably worn jeans and western shirt, Jake looked leaner, tougher, than Laurie remembered. And although he'd never been what she would term "cheerful," he used to smile every so often. Now it seemed as if that solemn scowl never left his face.

His mood didn't matter, she reminded herself. The only important thing was for Jake to do the job he'd been hired for, and so far his performance looked promising. He'd been at the Folly less than twelve hours, and already he was taking charge—inventorying the stock, making lists, setting priorities.

On one hand, his presence was comforting. Laurie was tired of dealing with the endless problems of running the Folly, and letting someone else take control of all her worries had a certain appeal. On the other hand, having Jake so close by was disturbing, setting off a chain reaction of awareness within her that had kept her awake last night, her body thrumming uncomfortably.

"Mommy, something stinks."

"What? Oh, no, the hash browns!" Laurie quickly pulled the cast-iron skillet off the burner and stirred the potatoes. A black layer had formed on the bottom of the pan, and she spent the next five minutes picking out the most burned pieces and dropping them into the trash.

That would teach her to stare out the window in the middle of cooking a meal, even if the view was more riveting than usual. She had to get hold of herself. She had to think of Jake as just another employee, not her former lover, or she wouldn't be able to function.

Wendy watched curiously from her booster chair, where she'd been sitting and drinking a glass of orange juice. "Did you burn something, Mommy?" she asked.

"Just a little. It's fine now," Laurie answered absently. "I think breakfast is ready. Would you go outside and ring the bell, please?"

Wendy scrambled out of her chair, eager to perform her favorite task. But she stopped at the door and looked at the four place settings on the table, her little brows drawn together as she put the pieces together. "Is Jake eating with us?"

"Yes, he is. And don't call him Jake, sweetie, call him Mr. Mercer."

"Why?"

"Because he's a grown-up, and children shouldn't call grown-ups by their first names."

"What about Maurice?"

"That's different," Laurie said. "He's practically part of the family."

"Then why can't he be my daddy?"

Laurie sighed. "He just can't be, okay? Now go ring the bell."

Wendy reached for the doorknob and twisted it, quietly chanting, "Mr. Merster, Mr. Merster." Just before she walked outside, she turned back to Laurie. "Jake's easier to say."

Laurie shook her head. She had a feeling that her efforts to keep Wendy and Jake away from each other would be in vain. The two seemed to have a sensitivity to one another, almost as if they both knew, on some subconscious level, that they were father and daughter. Last night, when Jake had pulled into the driveway with his truck loaded with the belongings he intended to move into the manager's house, Wendy had run out to greet him before Laurie could stop her. Then the child had jabbered nonstop as Jake had unloaded his belongings and taken them inside the little cottage.

Laurie had tried to take Wendy away, claiming that Jake should be left in peace while he was moving in, but Jake had insisted she stay. "Wendy's gonna be my number-one ranch hand, so we better get to know each other, right?" he'd said, tickling Wendy's chubby tummy.

Wendy had giggled, denying she was a ranch hand but obviously intrigued with the idea.

The old schoolhouse bell pealed as Wendy pulled strenuously on the rope. Laurie watched out the window as both Jake and Maurice looked up. Maurice waved to signal her that he'd heard, and Jake tipped his hat. Even at a distance, Laurie caught a glimpse of steel blue eyes—or maybe she only imagined them. Nonetheless, she shivered.

A few minutes later both men came into the kitchen. Jake's sleeves were rolled up, revealing sinewy, tanned forearms, and his hair was damp and slicked back, evidence that he'd washed up at the old pump before coming in for breakfast. Laurie tried not to stare as she served up scrambled eggs with green peppers, homemade biscuits and the slightly crusty hash browns.

"Smells good," Jake offered.

"Miz Laurie's turned into the best cook in the county," Maurice said, "though when she first came here she couldn't boil water. She learned quick, though."

Laurie's gaze locked with Jake's for an endless moment. How well she remembered his teasing her about her lack of cooking skills, insisting she ought to learn some domesticity if she wanted to keep her man home at night. And she had insisted, with a certain amount of suggestive body language, that she had other means of keeping her man's attention.

Looking at him now, she had a feeling that he, too, was remembering those peppery dialogues they used to have. She glanced away and took her chair, busying herself with her napkin.

"Mommy burneded the taters," Wendy announced.

"They are a bit browner than usual," Maurice said.

"Better crispy than raw," Jake added, taking a large bite of the hash browns.

Laurie stood abruptly. "You're right, they're too brown. I'll make some more," she said, moving to the refrigerator. "The potatoes are already shredded, I just have to fry them up. Won't take but—"

"Laurie, sit down," Jake interrupted. "The hash browns are fine."

"But it's no trouble."

"It's not necessary. Sit down."

Laurie bristled. How dare he order her around in her own house. Who was the boss here? Then she sighed. Jake could hardly be considered her employee when she wasn't paying him. He was trying to bail her out of a mess. And right now, he was being very tolerant of a less-than-satisfactory breakfast.

Why was she so concerned that breakfast be perfect, anyway?

Laurie reclaimed her chair, and the rest of the meal passed quietly, punctuated only by Wendy's oblivious chatter.

Maurice put his fork down with a gusty sigh of contentment and wiped his mouth with his napkin. "Well, now, that was a mighty fine breakfast."

Wendy giggled. "You always say that."

"It's always true. So, Sunshine, are you ready for another riding lesson this morning?"

Wendy's china blue eyes lit up with delight. "Can I, Mommy?"

Laurie started to say yes, but Jake interrupted. "Maurice won't have time for lessons this morning. We've got a full schedule."

"Surely he can take off thirty minutes..." The look Jake gave Laurie pinched off her objection.

Jake turned his attention to Wendy, whose cherubic face was wreathed in disappointment. "How about we have your lesson this afternoon?"

The little girl smiled again, though not quite as brightly as before. "Okay, Mr. Merster."

"Call me Jake."

"Mommy said not to."

Jake looked questioningly at Laurie.

"She's not supposed to call adults by their first names," Laurie said coolly. "It's the way I was raised, and she's being raised that way, too."

"Okay, fine." But Laurie didn't miss the conspiratorial wink he flashed at Wendy, and she suspected that no matter what her preferences, her daughter would be calling Jake "Jake."

Laurie stood and began clearing the dishes. "Wendy, honey, it's time to feed the cats. Ask Maurice to help you." She looked defiantly at Jake, daring him to countermand her orders.

He stared back, measuring, as he stood and donned his hat, but all he said was, "Thanks for breakfast."

"Wait a minute," she said, halting him at the door. "I'd like a word with you in private."

He pulled his Stetson back off and held it, fidgeting, until Maurice and Wendy were gone. "Yes, ma'am?" he asked politely.

"Don't use that patronizing tone with me. I'm still the boss here."

"I never said you weren't."

"Wendy's been taking riding lessons from Maurice twice a week for a month now, always right after breakfast. I don't appreciate your interfering with her routine."

"All I'm asking for is a slight postponement. I need Maurice's help this morning. Flash Lightning is due to arrive here any minute, and we don't even have a stall ready for him."

Laurie crossed her arms, wanting to object, but knowing that what Jake had said was perfectly sensible.

"Look, Laurie, if you want to see results around here, you're going to have to trust me. Cut me some slack. Let's try things my way."

"Trust you?" she repeated. "Trust is something you earn, Jake Mercer, and you haven't even begun to earn it yet."

"Then at least give me a chance to either succeed or fall on my face. I can't do the job if I don't have your support."

Laurie thought for a few moments. He wasn't asking for anything unreasonable. "Okay," she finally said, though grudgingly. "I guess I'm a little out of sorts this morning. I still have to call the vet and tell her my decision about Flash."

"I already did that. The surgery's scheduled for tomorrow."

Laurie's mouth dropped open. "That was not your decision to make!"

Jake took a step closer until he towered over her. "Anything concerning the running of this ranch or the finances or the stock is my decision to make. If we disagree on that, then you might as well fire me right now."

"I'm tempted!" She had to crane her neck to meet his electric blue gaze.

"Well?"

Her anger faltered. He knew damn well she wouldn't fire him. She needed him. Turning away, she said quietly, "All right, we're agreed. You have complete authority over the ranch. In return, I'll ask that in the future you show some sensitivity where Wendy's concerned. She doesn't have a father, and the time she spends with Maurice is important to both of them."

"Agreed. I'll make sure she gets her riding lesson this afternoon. Which horse does she ride, anyway?"

"Tosca." Laurie focused her gaze out the window toward the pasture. "The little red mare out there, grazing near the fence. She has a very sweet disposition."

"She's not so little, though."

Laurie resumed clearing the table, and to her surprise, Jake helped. "Wendy will grow into her. Meanwhile, I just want to get her used to horses so she won't be afraid of them the way I was."

"You're not anymore?" Jake asked. "I remember when you wouldn't even touch a horse. When we were kids, I couldn't get you on Paco's back for love or money. You wouldn't even ride behind me."

"I wasn't afraid of the horse, I was afraid of you," she quipped. When she realized what she'd said, she was horrified. How easy it was to step back into their old roles, even after all this time.

"Why were you afraid of me?" he asked, sounding genuinely curious.

She couldn't tell him the truth—that back in those days, when their mutual desires were first beginning to blossom, she was scared to death to go anywhere alone with him, afraid their innocent kisses would get out of control and she wouldn't be able to stop him or herself.

She chose not to answer his question. "I'll never be an expert rider, and certain horses still unnerve me," she said, "but I like to ride now and then."

"This I gotta see. I'll be riding out to check fences this afternoon. Why don't you come with me?"

"No, I'll be much too busy," she answered automatically.

"With what?" he challenged her. Their hands met under the faucet as they both went to rinse a dish at the same time.

Laurie jumped back as if she'd been branded. "With...with stuff, okay? I need to get my hair trimmed. And Wendy needs new clothes—she's outgrowing everything."

Jake dried his hands on a dishcloth. "Oh, that reminds me. You need to sit down and figure out what your monthly personal expenses are. I'll be putting you on an allowance."

Before she could even sputter an objection, he was gone.

Laurie was still carrying a full head of steam late that afternoon. Her frenzy of errands—which included a visit to her cousin Sadie, who'd provided two huge shopping bags of beautiful clothes her five-year-old had outgrown—had failed to improve her mood one bit. And since she knew it would be counterproductive to rail at Jake, she settled for the next best thing.

"Wendy, do you want to go visit Uncle Danny?"

Wendy clapped her hands. "Can I pet the bunnies? And the goats?"

"Sure." Danny kept hutches and pens out behind the store, where he dabbled with raising exotic lop ears and Angoras.

"Grandpa said maybe I can have a bunny for my birthday."

Way to go, Daddy. Wendy's fourth birthday wasn't for more than two months, and already she was anticipating her presents, especially the extravagant ones from her doting grandparents.

"Grandpa only said that because he doesn't have to feed the bunny and clean its cage," Laurie said. "Besides, you've got a barn full of kittens."

"And a horsey, too. Can I still ride today?"

"We'll be home in plenty of time for your nap and then a riding lesson afterward," Laurie said, hoping Wendy had been distracted from the subject of bunnies for the moment. She pulled into the parking lot of the

Feed Lot, Winnefred's biggest feed and livestock supply store, owned by her brother, Danny. Wendy wiggled impatiently as Laurie freed her from her car seat.

Laurie wished she could recapture that innocent glee for herself. To worry about nothing more important than riding lessons and whether she'd get a bunny for her birthday sounded so nice. Instead, she had to worry about Jake Mercer, and how she could possibly let Wendy's birthday slip by without him knowing about it.

"Hey, Sissy, what brings you here?"

Laurie closed the car door firmly and turned to look up at her older brother, who was loading a bag of dog food into the trunk of an elderly woman's Cadillac. Danny was blond and tanned and wholesome looking, the reigning bachelor of Winnefred. Too cute for his own good, Laurie thought uncharitably. His looks and charm let him get away with murder. Well, not this time.

"I came here because of Jake Mercer," Laurie said, then folded her arms and waited for the inevitable reaction.

But Danny merely nodded. He summoned a smile as he said goodbye to his customer, then focused his attention on Wendy. "I'll bet I know someone who'd like to see bunnies. Why don't you run inside and let Grandpa show you the new babies?"

Laurie nodded her permission and watched her daughter scamper off.

"Daddy's here today?" she asked, feeling trepidation set in. No telling how her father would react when he found out Jake was back in her life. Jake had never been Throckmore Branson's favorite person, dead or alive.

"He's been spending a lot of time here lately. Doesn't know quite what to do with himself since he retired. He's taken a real interest in the rabbits . . . but I guess you didn't come here to talk about rabbits.''

''No, I thought I'd discuss a different kind of rodent. Rats. One big rat in particular. How could you do it?'' she suddenly exploded. ''How could you not tell me that Jake was alive?''

A pained expression crossed Danny's face. ''Jake called the store this morning to get some information on feed deliveries to the Folly, so I knew we'd have this conversation sooner or later.''

''It should have been sooner—like three years ago!''

''You were in no shape to handle news like that three years ago. You'd just had a baby. You and Charlie were starting a family. Things were finally settling down for you. I didn't want to mess that up for you, and neither did Jake.''

''Dammit, I didn't need protecting. I could have handled it.''

''Maybe you could have, but what about Charlie? He loved you, you know. Always did.''

Laurie felt a stab of guilt. Jake's reappearance would have thrown Charlie for a loop, no doubt. He'd always been a bit insecure when it came to Laurie's feelings for Jake. She wouldn't have been able to stand seeing him hurt.

She cleared her throat. ''It's no easier now than it would have been then.''

''I know. I tried to talk Jake out of going to see you. But he kept insisting he had a debt to pay, or some such nonsense.''

A debt. That's all she was to him now.

''You're sorry he's back, then?'' Danny asked.

''I honestly don't know, Danny. But I do know one thing. If he hangs around for very long, he's going to find out about Wendy.'' She paused, waiting for a reaction. And when he didn't give one, she added, "You lied to him about that, didn't you?"

Danny stared down at the toes of his cowboy boots. "It seemed the best thing to do at the time. I knew if Jake found out he had a child, he'd go barging in to claim her, and what a mess that would have been."

"It's a terrible mess, all right. He's not stupid. He's going to figure it out sooner or later, and there'll be hell to pay."

"So help me, Laurie, I didn't think he'd ever come looking for you. I didn't know this thing would backfire like it has."

"Yeah, well, you should have thought about backfiring before you started telling lies. Now I'm stuck with Jake Mercer running my ranch, and I have a feeling it's going to get a whole lot worse before it gets better."

"Jake Mercer?"

Danny and Laurie both looked up to see their father standing not ten feet away, his jaw hanging open in stark surprise. The knot in Laurie's stomach tightened.

"Jake Mercer's alive? And he's at the Folly?"

Laurie nodded cautiously.

The older man turned abruptly and headed for his car.

"Daddy? Where are you going?"

"I'm gonna get my gun. And then I'm gonna go kill that son of a bitch."

"Easy, boy," Jake soothed the nervous stallion, holding on to his halter as he stroked his neck. "That's just Laurie's truck coming up the driveway. Lots of strange sights and sounds around here, I know, but you'll get used to it. And I think you'll like it. Especially once you get to know the ladies."

Already there were two mares in the adjacent paddock, prancing along the fence line, swishing their tails and trying to get Flash Lightning's attention. Ever since Flash had arrived two hours ago, his nostrils had been flaring. He was untried yet as a stud, but Jake had a feeling he'd know exactly how to woo the skittish fillies, just like his sire.

Jake had been grooming the horse in preparation for Laurie's return, wanting her first look at the Folly's new stud to be an impressive one. Losing Flash Senior's gene pool was an awful blow, he knew, and he hoped Flash Junior's presence would ease the pain a bit.

He watched as Laurie pulled the truck to a stop and got out. She looked tired, he thought. Maybe he only imagined it, but her shoulders seemed to droop a bit as she helped Wendy out of her car seat, then retrieved a couple of shopping bags from the back of the truck.

He released Flash's halter, pleased when the stallion trotted over to the fence to meet the fillies.

Laurie looked up and waved a lukewarm greeting as she gave Wendy a small package to carry, then sent her into the house with a pat on the rear.

"Come take a look at your new stud," Jake called out.

"In a minute," she called back distractedly. "I need to take these things inside and put Wendy down for her nap."

He didn't want her distracted. He wanted her full attention on Flash. He wanted her to ooh and aah, and maybe show a little gratitude for the effort he was putting forth.

He immediately squelched that thought. He wasn't doing this for her gratitude; he was doing it to settle an old debt. His own needs shouldn't even enter into the picture. Unfortunately one particular need was making itself known in a very visceral fashion. Every time he looked at Laurie, his gut tightened and his heart slammed against the wall of his chest. Other areas of his body tightened, too.

He'd known going into this that he would have to deal with some residual feelings for Laurie. He'd thought that if he kept reminding himself that they were both light-years away from the young, idealistic couple who'd almost been married four years ago, he could handle any errant physical yearnings.

He'd thought wrong. He hadn't counted on being so attracted to the woman Laurie had become.

"Where've you been all afternoon?" he asked as he approached her. "Buying out the stores?"

"You don't have to scowl at me like that. I wasn't out emptying the Folly's bank accounts. Most of these clothes are hand-me-downs from my cousin Sadie. She has a little girl just a bit older than Wendy."

"I didn't mean to scowl." He was, however, undeniably disturbed—not by the idea of Laurie spending money, but by the thought of Wendy wearing some other child's cast-offs. "Look, I won't deny the money's going to be tight around here for a while. But I don't want your little girl to go lacking. If she needs anything—"

"You just said this morning you were going to put me on an allowance," Laurie interrupted. "I thought you'd be pleased that I'm saving money."

"The allowance will be enough to cover your needs. Did you get your hair cut?" he asked, inspecting her hair for any minute change.

She ran a nervous hand through the sun-bright strands, not quite shoulder length. "I didn't have time."

"Good. I don't want you to cut it," he said before thinking.

"I don't recall asking you," she said tartly. "Furthermore, where I go and what I do with my afternoons are none of your business. Your authority includes the ranch, but it doesn't include me."

"I liked your hair long," he said softly, ignoring her angry outburst.

"Yeah, well, you wouldn't like it if you'd had a baby pulling on it all the time. I had to cut it for my own survival."

"Wendy's old enough that she wouldn't pull on it now. You should grow it out again."

"I like it short," she said, her ire mounting. "You're here to run a ranch, not be a beauty consultant."

"You don't need a beauty consultant."

She blushed a becoming shade of peach. "I have things to do," she said, starting toward the house. But after a couple of steps she turned. "Since you're so interested, I spent a good portion of my afternoon trying to convince my father not to run over here with his shotgun and fill your rump full of lead."

Jake couldn't help but grimace. "Ah. I take it you told your daddy I'm back?"

"By accident. Now the whole town knows, or it will within a few hours. Daddy and I had a rather noisy discussion about you while standing outside the Feed Lot."

Well, hell. Throckmore Branson had never made it a secret that he didn't approve of Jake marrying his youngest daughter. He was a formidable man to have as an enemy. "Everyone would have found out sooner or later," Jake said with more pragmatism than he felt. "There'll be a few wagging tongues, some speculation, some ancient history resurrected, but it'll die down before we know it."

"I hope you're right. I don't mind people gossiping about you or me, but I won't stand by and let it hurt Wendy."

"Wendy?" Jake repeated, puzzled. "She's just a child. She doesn't have anything to do with me or why I'm here. I don't think you have to worry about that."

Laurie closed her eyes for a moment, and when she opened them, they were expressionless. "I'm sure you're right."

Four

Laurie was trembling by the time she made it inside the house. This wasn't going to work. Every time Jake so much as mentioned Wendy's name, Laurie had to struggle to control her reaction. If he didn't guess the truth just by her peculiar behavior, surely someone else would clue him in.

The question was, should she tell him now and get it over with, or should she wait and hope he moved on before he discovered the truth?

If he discovered Wendy was his daughter, and that Laurie had kept that fact from him, he might never speak to her again. On the other hand, she couldn't envision him abandoning his daughter. She would never be rid of him—their lives would be inexorably connected. Neither possibility thrilled her.

By the time she'd put Wendy down for her nap, Laurie felt more in control. She stored her purchases, then went outside to have a look at the new Wonder Stud, which she'd only caught a brief glimpse of a few minutes earlier.

As she approached the paddock, her breath caught in her throat. Jake hadn't exaggerated. Flash Lightning was the spitting image of Flash in the Pan—but younger, leaner, still full of the fire that burns in a young stallion.

She climbed up on the fence rail to have a better look. Even placidly grazing, as he was now, he emanated a certain vitality that thrilled her to the bone. What pretty colts and fillies this horse would make.

Gradually Laurie became aware of a presence standing next to her. Without even looking she knew it was Jake. Like the stallion, he had a certain heat and vitality of his own, a vibration that meshed and mingled with hers.

"Didn't I tell you he was something?" Jake held up a carrot and whistled softly. The horse raised his head and pricked up his ears. At the sight of the carrot he trotted over.

That was when Laurie noticed the limp. Flash Lightning strongly favored his right front leg.

"Oh, Jake, what a shame that such a beautiful animal has to be disabled."

"It would have been a worse shame if he'd been turned into glue."

Laurie grimaced at the thought. She'd never had to deal with glue factories or dog food companies before. Charlie had been a good businessman, but he'd had a soft heart when it came to his horses. He'd usually managed to sell off the older ones as pleasure mounts, almost always to kids looking for a gentle first horse.

There were a few old mares he'd simply turned out to pasture, to live their last days happily grazing.

"Did it cost a lot to save him?" Laurie asked.

"Enough."

"What made you do it? I mean, most people wouldn't spend thousands of dollars in vet bills on a horse that can never be ridden."

"I don't know. I guess I couldn't stand the thought of him being destroyed."

Laurie considered his answer. "Possibly, but I've never pictured you as the softhearted type."

"Maybe I've changed."

She couldn't argue with that. The Jake she'd known four years ago had been a simple man. He'd been sure of what was right and wrong, dedicated to his job with the Marshals Service, and ready to settle down with a wife and kids. No complications. Everything was black-and-white.

This new Jake was more complex—shades of gray. It was almost as if his experience with the LaBarbas in Costa Rica had added a whole new dimension. Or perhaps four years ago she'd been too immature and too infatuated to see beyond the surface. Laurie found him more fascinating than ever, and part of her wanted to get beneath his skin and discover the real Jake Mercer.

"Will the limp ever get any better?" Laurie asked hopefully, cautiously stroking Flash Lightning's neck. She was pretty sure she knew what Jake's answer would be.

"No. But he still has some good genes to pass along to Birkett's Folly."

Laurie could see that. As the horse snuffled the carrot out of Jake's hand, Laurie continued to rub his neck, all the while keeping a wary eye on his big teeth. Some of the stallions she'd encountered were mean as pit vipers.

"You don't have to be afraid of him," Jake said. "He's a bit livelier than his old sire, but every bit as gentle. Just give him a treat and he's your friend for life." He pulled another carrot from his pocket.

Laurie took the carrot Jake offered her and held it out gingerly on the palm of her hand. Flash Lightning lifted the morsel daintily into his mouth, barely touching her. "He is gorgeous," Laurie murmured. "So when do we try him out?"

"I'm planning to let him have a go with that little dun mare who put Flash Senior out of commission—I'll hobble her this time. She's still ready."

"You think I made a good choice with her?" Laurie asked. "She's all the way from Tennessee, and none from her line have been bred to Flash Senior. I remember Charlie talking about how you had to be careful not to create too many foals from the same gene pool."

Laurie didn't add that she'd found some old notes of Charlie's indicating his plans for the delicate dun quarter-horse mare, which he'd bought as a yearling shortly before his stroke.

For some reason, it was important that Jake not think she was a total idiot when it came to running the ranch.

"I think she's an excellent choice," Jake said. "You and Maurice were on the right track with the breeding program, from what I can tell. The Folly's biggest problem is a cash-flow crunch."

"Tell me about it," she said, ridiculously pleased with his little scrap of praise. Then she added glumly, "And not even you can spin cash out of thin air."

He winked at her. "You might be surprised."

Was that the hint of a smile she saw on his face? Oh, what this man did to all her best intentions. The warm April sun and the smell of spring grass and horses, not to mention Jake's nearness, made her feel woozy. She hopped down from the fence railing before she fell. At the same time, Jake took a step forward, perhaps intending to give her a hand. She landed right in his arms.

Time stopped and all the air whooshed out of her lungs as long-repressed memories assaulted her. Jake steadied her, holding her a fraction longer than was necessary or proper, and she made absolutely no move to escape him. In that moment of weakness, she easily could have let him kiss her.

He didn't, of course. Thank goodness one of them had some sense.

"You okay?"

"It's the sun," she improvised, stepping away to put some distance between them. "And I shouldn't have skipped lunch, I guess. Made me a little dizzy. I'm fine now." She struggled for something to say that would put them back on a firm business footing. "So when do we introduce the happy couple?" she asked, nodding toward Flash.

"The sooner the better," Jake replied. "When it comes to romance, delaying never solves anything."

For the second time in as many minutes, all the air escaped from Laurie's lungs, leaving her to gape wordlessly like a landed fish. By the time she found her breath, Jake had turned and walked away.

The next day Laurie was too preoccupied with Flash Senior's surgery to worry much about Jake. Maurice had loaded the old stallion into the trailer before breakfast and driven him over to the vet's. Laurie had fidgeted all morning until Dr. Calloway had called to tell her that Flash had come through with flying colors.

But when the horse had returned to the Folly late that afternoon, Laurie had thought he looked awful—dull-eyed, listless, stumbling a bit as he was unloaded from the trailer.

"It's just the tranquilizers," said Jake, who'd gone over himself to pick up the stallion-turned-gelding from the vet and bring him back. He'd obviously seen Laurie's alarm and was trying to reassure her. "Also, the doc shot him up with painkillers and antibiotics, and she gave me some more doses to use later. He'll be fine in a couple of days. Meanwhile, we're supposed to keep him quiet in his stall."

Laurie took hold of Flash's halter. "I'll take him into the barn," she volunteered. "And if you'll show me how and when to give him his medicine, I can do that, too. You and Maurice probably have more important things to do than coddle an old invalid. Right, Flash?"

The horse didn't respond at all to her voice.

"Can you give a horse an injection?" Jake asked.

Laurie made a face. "Uh, no. Maurice always handles that kind of stuff. But I could learn," she said with not much enthusiasm.

Jake shook his head. "Never mind, I'll do it. If you'd keep an eye on the old guy, you know, check in on him from time to time, that would be a big help."

Laurie felt suddenly like a little kid being humored by the grown-ups. How did Jake always manage to ferret out her weaknesses and make her feel incompetent? With a sigh she led the compliant Flash into the barn.

The horse truly worried her when he walked into his stall and then wouldn't turn and face out. Instead he stood with his head in the corner.

"C'mon, Flash, at least look at me. It's not as bad as you think. I know you're embarrassed 'cause you're not a big macho stud anymore. But you can still enjoy life. You can play with the fillies anytime you want—no more keeping you locked up. And we'll go for long rides, just you and me. As soon as you're up to it, of course."

She wondered when that would be as she went to the tack room to get some rags and liniment. She would give the old guy a nice, gentle rubdown. That should put him in a better mood.

Jake came into the barn to get a lead rope, intending to give his stallion some exercise, but he stopped when he heard Laurie's voice. Who in the hell was she talking to? Then he realized the conversation was decidedly one-sided. She was talking to Flash in the Pan.

He couldn't stop himself from listening to her unguarded monologue. Her obvious affection for the animal touched something deep inside him. He recalled times when she'd spoken to him with that same soft lilt in her voice, a voice full of love. And he'd been too caught up with his manly pride to reciprocate.

He'd loved her. He'd even told her so a time or two, when it seemed as if she might leave him if he didn't. But mostly he'd been content to simply sit back and bask in the warmth of Laurie's love.

He'd been so intent on the LaBarbas back in those days, so devoted to tracking them down and putting their whole drug-dealing clan behind bars, that he didn't have much time to devote to Laurie. But she hadn't seemed to mind. She'd understood, better than his own family, what drove him. He was a lawman first, and she'd accepted that.

It pained him now to think about what he'd taken so easily for granted. Laurie was always there for him, had always been there, and he'd never thought to question her devotion. He'd never envisioned life without her.

It tortured him to think about what he'd lost—or rather, what he'd carelessly thrown away—that clear, hot morning, the day he was supposed to take Laurie as his wife. And for what? Thirteen months of living hell as LaBarba's prisoner. Ernesto LaBarba had been killed when the Marshals Service wanted him alive, and Juan had gotten away, his organization in shambles but not ruined for good. In fact, rumors in the law enforcement community had surfaced lately, hinting that Juan was back in business in his old territory.

If only Jake had that day to live over again...

But he didn't. He'd made his choices, and now he had to live with them. He'd lost Laurie to another man, another life. And he'd best not even think about trying to get her back, although it was hard not to entertain fantasies when he could hear her softly crooning.

Good Lord, was she actually singing a lullaby?

He'd had no idea she was so emotionally attached to Flash. That made what he had to tell her twice as difficult. He cleared his throat and clomped his boots against the packed earth of the barn floor as he approached, not wanting to startle or embarrass her.

The singing stopped abruptly.

"Hey, how's the old boy doing?" Jake asked, leaning his elbows on the top of the stall door.

Laurie was standing behind the horse, combing out his tail. From the looks of things, she had thoroughly groomed Flash. His coat was clean and shiny, and his flowing mane had been tied into a series of little braids.

"He's not very happy," Laurie said glumly. "I thought maybe if I spruced him up a bit he'd feel better about himself."

The only thing that kept Jake from laughing out loud was that Laurie was a hundred percent sincere. "Laurie, Flash isn't a human being. I don't think animals have self-esteem problems."

"This one does," she said with utter conviction. "He's never been anything but a champion and a stud. I'm afraid he's feeling useless."

"He's not feeling anything except postsurgical pain and dullness from the drugs," Jake argued. "He's a horse."

"You obviously don't know him like I do. He's a special horse. He understands everything that goes on around him."

"And I suppose he understands what we're saying, too?" Jake asked, intending only to tease her.

Laurie threw him a hard look. "Maybe not the words. But he can hear the feelings behind the words. See how he tossed his head just now? He knows we're arguing and he doesn't like it."

"We're not arguing," Jake objected. "We're merely having a friendly discussion." But he had a feeling they were getting ready to argue—big-time—as soon as he announced his latest decision.

"Whatever," Laurie said. "Flash can sense hostility."

"Must be yours he's sensing, then, because I'm not feeling the slightest bit hostile." In fact, Jake was feeling distinctly turned on just watching Laurie work on Flash's tail, her graceful hands gently pulling out the knots and rubbing the horse's rump reassuringly, her full lower lip caught in her teeth as she concentrated.

He'd almost kissed her when she'd stumbled into him earlier, but common sense had prevailed. If he tried something like that, she would probably order him off the ranch so fast his head would spin, and all his effort would be for nothing. No matter, he still wanted to kiss her—and more. The strength of the sudden wave of lust he felt took him by surprise.

Without warning, Flash stretched his neck out and nipped Jake on the arm, pinching the skin just enough to smart.

"Ouch!" He jerked his arm out of reach and rubbed the tender spot.

Laurie looked up. "What?"

"He bit me," Jake said, thoroughly offended. It had been years since he'd allowed a horse to get away with that kind of behavior.

"Who bit you?"

"Who do you think? Your paragon of a horse." And if Jake didn't know better, he'd think Flash had read his mind and had been reprimanding him for his lusty thoughts about his mistress.

"Don't be ridiculous," Laurie said, returning her attention to a particularly difficult knot. "Flash has never bitten anyone."

Jake could swear the damn horse was smirking, as if he knew Jake would never convince Laurie that he'd been nipped. He decided not to try.

"Look, Laurie, there's something we need to talk about."

"What is it?" she asked without looking up, giving Flash's tail one final whisk of the comb.

"It's about Flash. I found a buyer for him."

Laurie's hands stilled. "I thought you were going to let him stand at stud for the Folly. That was our agreement."

It took Jake only a moment to realize Laurie had misunderstood. She thought he was referring to Flash

Junior. "No, no," he said quickly. "Our agreement still stands. I'm talking about this Flash."

For several heartbeats, all Laurie could do was stare in shocked silence. "You're going to sell Flash in the Pan?" she finally managed in a weak voice.

"There's really no other choice. This is a breeding farm, and there's no place for an aging gelding. He's become a liability, Laurie. You haven't seen the final vet bill. I've been offered a very decent price for the horse, and I don't see any reason not to accept."

"I'll give you a reason," Laurie said as she picked up her grooming tools with angry, jerky movements. "I won't let you sell him."

Jake shook his head. He should have seen this coming. Laurie was far too emotional when it came to the running of a ranch. "Laurie, be reasonable."

"I am being perfectly reasonable," she said, shrilly enough to cause Flash's ears to perk up. She barreled her way out of the stall, and Jake had to jump out of the way of the door to avoid being hit.

"Didn't we have this discussion yesterday?" he asked. "Didn't you agree to try things my way for a while?"

"Yesterday you weren't talking about selling Flash."

When he saw the sheen of tears in her eyes, he softened. "Look, Laurie, I know you're fond of the horse. But this is a business decision."

"And feelings always take a back seat to business, is that it? Why am I not surprised? Isn't that the way you've always operated?"

Abruptly Jake realized they were talking about a lot more than the sale of a horse. "Let's leave ancient history out of this discussion, shall we?"

"Why should we? Since ancient history is the whole reason you're here—to repay a debt, you said. Well, you aren't going to repay any debts by selling my horse. All you're doing is proving that my father was right about you. You're bound and determined to do your duty—as you see it—and you don't care whose feelings get trampled on in the process."

"For God's sake, Laurie, I didn't leave you standing at the altar on purpose," he said, abandoning the argument about Flash in favor of what was really on both their minds. "I didn't deliberately step in front of that bullet."

"But you did decide to go on a raid the morning of our wedding," she said, her eyes filling with tears. She dashed them away angrily. "On the single most important day of our lives, when you should have been thinking about love and family and the future we'd talked about, you decided it was more important to play macho man. You had a couple of hours to spare before you were due at the church, and you decided to squeeze in a dangerous raid on a murdering drug lord."

Her voice escalated in volume as the bitter tirade continued. "You knew damn well that a million things could have gone wrong, including your getting hurt. You knew damn well that you might not make it to the church on time, and you didn't care. You don't care about anybody but yourself. You left me alone to explain to a church full of people—the whole damn town, for God's sake—that you'd abandoned me and then gotten your fool self killed!"

Jake had nothing to say in his defense. At the time, he'd honestly believed that the raid would come off clean, and he couldn't imagine telling his boss that he wouldn't participate, not when he'd been leading the LaBarba investigation for three years. But he hadn't taken Laurie's feelings into consideration. Like always, he'd just assumed that she would be there for him when he got back, that they'd get married one way or another.

Laurie continued to lambaste him, and he just stood there and took it, figuring he had it coming. She'd been holding on to this anger for four...no, closer to five years. It was about time she got to express it.

At some point she ran out of steam, and she fell silent, tears streaming down her cheeks, her chest heaving as she took in one labored breath after another, her sobs choking her.

"Laurie," he said softly, "I wouldn't deliberately hurt you for anything in the world. But obviously I did hurt you, and I'm sorry. God, I'm so sorry." Before he could think about it he folded her into his arms and held her tightly. She was stiff at first, but gradually she relaxed, warm and soft against him. The front of his shirt grew wet with her tears.

"You know what the worst part of it was?" she said, her voice muffled against his chest.

"No, what?"

"I was so angry at you for leaving me alone. I even hated you for a while. But I couldn't tell anyone that. You were dead, for God's sake. You died in the line of duty, defending honor and decent people against scum like the LaBarbas, and suddenly you became St. Jake. Even my father said nice things about you. I couldn't utter a single word against you without feeling like a complete witch, so I didn't. I played the part of the grieving bride and I never let anyone know how I really felt."

"I bet it feels pretty good to yell at me now," he said. And it felt better than pretty good to hold her again. He buried his fingers in her hair, reveling in the feel of the silky strands, and remembering. How could he have stayed away for so long?

"As a matter of fact, it feels damn good."

"Do it some more, then. Get everything off your chest."

She looked up at him with those watery blue eyes, and he was lost. "It's kind of hard to yell at someone when they've got their arms around you."

The way she was looking at him so expectantly, with her head tilted just so and her lips slightly parted, he had no choice. Even knowing he was digging his own grave, he dipped his head and captured her mouth with his.

She responded instantly, coming alive in his arms. He tasted the salt of her tears and smelled the clean, green-apple fragrance of her shampoo, the same shampoo she'd been using for years. She made no protest when he invaded her mouth with his tongue, exploring, tasting, remembering.

His hands wandered over her back and down to cup the firm swell of her hip. To his surprise, instead of protesting she pulled herself more tightly against him, deliberately pressing herself against his arousal.

Her kisses had always stirred him, but he couldn't recall ever getting so turned on so fast before. Then again, he didn't remember Laurie as anything but timid when it came to sex. He wondered if Charlie had taught her to kiss like that.

The alien thought immediately cooled his ardor. Laurie wasn't his anymore. Not two months after his supposed death she'd married another man and made a life with him, a family.

At about that time Laurie seemed to come to her senses. As if by some prearranged signal they both abruptly broke off the kiss. Laurie stepped back and, to

Jake's amazement, she laughed out loud. "I can't believe we just did that," she said, her voice taking on a slightly hysterical note.

Jake could believe it. That kiss had been a long time in coming.

She put a hand to her forehead, still looking a bit dazed. "I don't know which felt better, yelling at you or kissing you."

He had to chuckle at her honesty. "I know which one I liked better."

"I really didn't mean—"

"Me, neither. Enough said."

"I'm still opposed to selling Flash. You can't change my mind with a few words of understanding and a kiss."

Jake's spine stiffened. "That hadn't occurred to me," he said, stung that she would even think he'd been trying to soften her up when he'd held her and comforted her. Did she really think he was that conniving? "I don't know why you're suspicious of every move I make. The whole reason I'm here at the Folly is to help you."

She eyed him skeptically. "Oh, really? Your motives are entirely altruistic, is that it? Nothing to gain at all?"

He looked down at the pointed toes of his boots. Okay, maybe she had a point. He wouldn't be here if he wasn't trying to assuage his own guilt. And maybe, just maybe, a part of him wanted to stake a new claim on Laurie.

The scariest thing was Laurie apparently knew his motives better than he did. She'd already figured out that he was interested in her as more than a charity case.

"Can we get back to discussing Flash?" he said. "I haven't even told you about the buyer. You might like—"

"You can't sell him, and that's final," she said, once again bristling like a porcupine. Damn, her moods changed faster than he could keep up with—and maybe he shouldn't even try. She turned to leave, but he wasn't going to let her have the last word.

"If that's your final decision, I'll pack up tonight and leave in the morning."

She stopped. "You can't—"

"Don't worry, I'll leave Flash Lightning here. In fact, I'll give him to you. He's no use to me. What good's a lame stud without a herd of mares?" He turned and strode away before he could change his mind.

Five

She was glad Jake was leaving, Laurie told herself as she ran water for Wendy's bath. It was obvious they weren't going to see eye to eye on anything at the Folly.

And then there was that stupid kiss. What on earth had gotten into her? The way she'd clung to Jake, opening up to him like a sex-starved wanton, no telling what he thought of her. And then she'd had the nerve to accuse him of having some hidden agenda, when she was the one who wasn't clear on why she'd allowed him to come to the Folly in the first place.

She'd been lonely for too long, that was all. Jake had caught her at a vulnerable moment and hormones had taken over. Now that she was aware of the danger, she wouldn't let it happen again. After all, if she got it into her head to get involved with a man, she certainly wouldn't choose Jake Mercer again. Not a chance.

Still, Laurie couldn't feel satisfied about the way she'd left things with Jake. She should have been happy that he was going away and leaving his beautiful stallion behind, but instead she was definitely . . . unsettled.

As she helped Wendy into the tub, she considered the future she'd elected for herself. She and Maurice could go on as they had before, now that she knew they'd been on the right track with the breeding program. There were three foals due next month, and two of them already had potential buyers. And with Flash Lightning standing at stud, the Folly could start generating income.

But despite such optimism, she felt awful about what she'd said to Jake. Perhaps he was a bit single-minded when it came to business and duty and all that, but to say that he cared for no one but himself was an out-and-out lie.

She hadn't been able to keep herself from saying it, though. All of that hurt from the past had welled up unexpectedly until she'd felt compelled to hurt Jake back. And she'd succeeded, if the look on his face had been any indication.

"Mommy, why didn't Ja—Mr. Merster eat dinner with us?" Wendy asked as Laurie shampooed her hair.

Laurie thought about the empty place setting at the dinner table and felt a twinge of guilt. "He was probably busy packing, sweetheart. He's moving out in the morning."

"Oh. But he just got here."

"I know, but things aren't working out like we'd all hoped."

"What things?"

How did one explain this to a three-year-old? "Mr. Mercer and I found out we had different ideas about how to run the ranch. We can't work together."

Wendy scrunched up her face the way she did when she was thinking hard about something. "You can't get along?"

"Yes, that's right."

"Then why don't you go in 'time-out' and think about it?" Wendy offered brightly. "That's what we do at my school when we get in fights and stuff. Then we 'pologize and share."

If only it were that easy. Laurie smiled and brushed a soapy curl off Wendy's forehead. "Jake and I have been in 'time-out' for a long, long time," she said. "We've both thought and thought about it, and we've decided we can't work out our argument. So it's best if he leaves."

Wendy frowned, clearly disturbed by this anomaly. She'd been taught, by her preschool teacher and by Laurie herself, that disagreements can and should be worked out.

After putting Wendy to bed, Laurie finished cleaning the kitchen, but she couldn't get her mind off Jake. Had they even tried to overcome their difference of opinion? Certainly Jake had explained his reasons for wanting to sell Flash. But she hadn't offered any similarly sensible argument for keeping the gelding.

As for the rest of their argument, she'd really been out of line bringing up their wedding day. Like Jake had said, that was ancient history and it had no place in today's dealings.

As she dried her hands on a dishcloth, she came to a decision. She'd behaved badly this afternoon, and she would have to apologize. She would also try to convince Jake to stay on. The Folly needed him.

After checking to see that Wendy was asleep, Laurie slipped out of the house and made her way to the barn to check on Flash. From there it was just a short distance to Jake's cottage. The evening had cooled down considerably, and by the time she made it to the barn she was wishing she'd put on a sweater.

To her relief, Flash was looking a bit more alert than he had earlier. He whinnied when he caught her scent, and she spent several minutes petting him and trying to feed him treats, which he politely declined. His lack of appetite concerned her, but at least he was responding to her now.

When she'd done all she could for him, she gave him one final pat, screwed up her courage and headed for Jake's cottage. The bedroom light was still on. When she reached the front porch, she raised her fist to knock, but before she could make contact, the door jerked open.

She gasped and jumped back, and Jake screeched to a halt just before barreling into her.

"Laurie?" He clearly didn't sound pleased to find her lurking on his front porch.

"H-hi. I was just about to knock." She felt as awkward as when she'd been a teenager, that first time she'd realized she felt something other than annoyance for Jake Mercer. The light cotton shorts and sleeveless top she'd put on to give Wendy her bath suddenly seemed much too brief, and the fact that Jake was shirtless didn't help matters.

"What can I do for you?" he asked, polite and cool.

"I . . . can I come in?"

"Actually, I was coming outside for some fresh air." He sidled past her and went to sit on the porch railing. "We can talk out here."

She would rather have not. It was dark on the front porch, too intimate, and reminiscent of all those evenings she and Jake had spent sitting in her parents' porch swing back in their courting days. But it appeared Jake wasn't giving her an option.

She backed up against the wall a safe distance from him. "I'm not happy with how we left things this afternoon," she began. "I don't want you to leave."

"I don't want to leave," he admitted, his gaze focused out into the darkness. "But I can't stay here and manage things if you're going to hamstring me, second-guess every decision I make. I can't work under those conditions."

"I understand that. But you really threw me for a loop when you said you were going to sell Flash. You can do whatever you want with the rest of the stock. But Flash...well, he's not just a commodity. He's more like a pet."

"Why's he so special to you?" Jake asked, suddenly spearing her with those penetrating blue eyes of his.

Laurie hadn't intended to go into the full explanation, but maybe her stand would make more sense to Jake if she did. "Flash in the Pan is my horse. Charlie gave him to me as a wedding present—to prove he was really committed. He said the Folly was nothing without its champion stud, and he wanted to show me that...that he truly believed we'd be together forever. I was so honored by his gift that I was determined I would get over my fear of horses. I learned to ride on Flash. He's always been my mount. Flash is my last link with Charlie, I guess," she finished lamely.

Jake was silent for a long time, making Laurie wish she hadn't gone into quite so much detail. The story had made it sound as if she'd been deeply in love with Charlie and that she still pined away for him.

"What about Wendy?" Jake asked.

"What about her?" Laurie asked warily.

"She's your link with Charlie." Jake sounded just a little bit defensive—and maybe slightly envious. That pricked at Laurie's conscience. She should tell Jake that Wendy was his daughter. But not now. Oh, Lord, not now! She had too much other emotional sludge to deal with.

"Of course, you're right about Wendy," she said. "I'm just trying to explain why I'm oversentimental about Flash. Who is it that wants to buy him?"

Jake seemed to relax a bit. He swung one jean-clad leg back and forth as he explained. "I ran into Will Patterson at the vet's office. He wants to buy Flash for his son, Brandon."

"Little Brandon?" Laurie couldn't picture it.

"Brandon's eleven and not so little. He weighs almost as much as I do and he's growing fast. He wants to learn competitive calf roping. He needs a big mount, but a gentle one. Flash seems perfect."

Laurie knew the Pattersons well. They kept a nice little stable with a couple of pleasure horses less than a mile from the Folly. Flash would be well cared for. And he would probably enjoy the competition and exercise he would get calf roping. Laurie never did any of that type of riding.

"Would they mind if I came and visited?" she asked, knowing that with her question she was dangerously close to capitulating.

"I'm sure they wouldn't."

"And when Flash gets too old to ride, or if he gets sick, will they agree to put him out to pasture and let him go naturally?"

"I can work that into the deal," Jake said with growing enthusiasm, obviously smelling victory. "And I didn't tell you the best part. The Pattersons have a

Shetland pony mare that their youngest has outgrown, and they're willing to include the pony in the deal.''

''You mean, for Wendy?'' Laurie said, delighted with the idea.

Jake nodded. ''The way she teeters on big ol' Tosca's back scares me to death.''

''Wait a minute. Does a Shetland pony have any more business on a breeding farm than an old gelding? I mean, won't she be an expense we can't afford?''

''She won't eat much,'' Jake said, sounding like a little boy who's brought home a stray puppy.

Laurie was shocked at the change in his attitude. A few minutes earlier, it had seemed he couldn't care less about her sentimental attachment to Flash. But when it came to Wendy, the big jerk had a heart as soft as a marshmallow. Laurie wasn't sure how she felt about that.

It didn't take her long to come to a decision about selling Flash. For some reason, Jake's plan sounded quite reasonable now. She would miss the old horse, but as long as he was happy, that was what mattered most. ''All right, then, you negotiate the deal and I'll sign the papers,'' she said grudgingly. ''Now, you're not really leaving in the morning, are you?''

He scratched his chin and pretended to consider her question carefully. ''Are we going to have these stormy arguments every time I—''

''No, no, I swear, Jake, I'll leave it all in your hands. I'd like it if you'd keep me informed, but I won't second-guess your decisions.''

''Then I guess I'll go unpack.'' He hopped off the porch railing and brushed tantalizingly close to her as he moved toward the door. She caught a trace of his scent—

he smelled of soap and leather and horses. As he passed, she took a deep breath.

"Jake?"

He stopped. "What?"

"About what happened this afternoon . . ."

He had to know what she was referring to, but he continued to look at her, waiting for her to explain, his eyes sparkling with deviltry.

Damn him! "The kiss," she said, barely breathing the words.

"What about it?"

Her mouth went as dry as a hot July afternoon. "It was a mistake . . . wasn't it?"

One corner of his mouth lifted in what might have passed for a smile, but he didn't answer her. He just turned and walked into the cabin, letting the door slam behind him.

Laurie called herself ten kinds of fool for asking Jake to stay.

Jake lay awake that night, pondering the accusations Laurie had made earlier. Why was he here? Was it to help Laurie or soothe his conscience—or get her into bed and prove she still had feelings for him?

Given the fact that his body was still thrumming from the memory of that kiss, he couldn't deny that he harbored some ulterior motives. He wanted Laurie and he intended to have her. Just the sight of her in that skimpy shorts outfit, illuminated by a shaft of light coming through the doorway, had made his whole body go hard. He'd been grateful for the fact that he'd been hidden in semidarkness.

As for his wanting to sell Flash Senior, he had to admit that his reasons weren't entirely for business purposes. Maurice had told him, before Laurie had, that the stallion had been her wedding present from Charlie. Knowing that Flash Senior must be a constant reminder of Charlie, Jake had found the prospect of selling him much more attractive. The sale had seemed fated when he'd run into Will Patterson at the vet's, and with no prompting at all Will had expressed an interest in buying Flash for his son.

Now Jake began second-guessing himself. Was he causing Laurie more pain than was necessary by selling Flash? Was he, on some subconscious level, punishing her for marrying Charlie, for loving Charlie?

Pride swelled in Laurie's chest as she stood on the fence railing and watched her daughter riding her new Shetland pony. Wendy's face was serious as she gripped the reins in her left hand, doggedly resisting the urge to grab on to the horn of the miniature saddle. In less than a week she'd made tremendous progress, now that she had a mount her own size. Maurice kept the pony on a lead rope, but Wendy was actually in control.

Laurie had put on a brave face the day Will and Brandon Patterson had come to pick up Flash in the Pan. Will had told her she was welcome to visit anytime, and that of course she could take the old gelding for a ride now and then. Flash, always a good-natured horse, had seemed eager to please when Brandon had ridden him around the corral for the first time. The boy was clearly ecstatic, showering his new horse with gentle pats and words of encouragement, and Laurie had been convinced she was doing the right thing.

Still, she would miss the old guy. A lump had formed in her throat as the horse trailer pulled down the driveway and away. But the new little addition to the Folly's stable took some of the sting away.

June Bug was the cutest, shiniest brown pony Laurie had ever seen. And although Shetland ponies weren't known for their gentle dispositions, this one was an exception. She all but crawled into Laurie's lap in her quest for affection, stuck her nose in various pockets looking for treats and generally endeared herself to anyone who saw her.

When Wendy had come home from her weekly preschool that afternoon and had seen the pony for the first time she'd been speechless with delight. The two of them had instantly bonded, and riding lessons had taken on a whole new meaning for Wendy.

All in all, things had been running smoothly over the past week. One of the mares had dropped her foal, a beautifully marked paint colt, and Jake had already lined up a buyer. He'd also picked up a gorgeous black brood mare at an auction for a song, beginning the long process of replenishing the Folly's herd.

Only one little black cloud marred Laurie's optimistic horizon, and that was Jake. Or rather, the way she acted around Jake, the way she felt. She was in no way remaining impersonal and businesslike toward him, as she'd hoped. Sometimes she'd feel herself tingling all over, and she would look up to find Jake staring at her. Sometimes she caught herself staring at him, lost in thoughts about the past and fantasies of a future she didn't dare hope for.

The whole thing made her nervous, and she belatedly wished she'd put some sort of limit on the time he would spend at the Folly. If they'd agreed to a six-month term, for example, she could count the days until he would move on. That would at least put an end in sight. As it stood now, she was looking ahead to having Jake around indefinitely.

At least she'd come up with a solution to one problem. Laurie's parents were taking a trip to the Grand Canyon, and they wanted to take Wendy with them. The trip just happened to coincide with Wendy's birthday.

It wasn't that Laurie wanted to keep Wendy's parentage a secret from Jake forever. In fact, the more she saw them together—a distressingly frequent occurrence these days—the more she realized that Jake deserved to know that Wendy was his daughter. But before she told him, she had to be sure she could convince him not to go public with his newfound status as a father. She could not bear to think of Charlie's role in Wendy's life being diminished that way. Even though Wendy couldn't remember Charlie, Laurie was determined that she would grow up knowing what a fine man he was, so she could be proud of her daddy.

Jake wasn't going to mess that up.

"She's going to be a helluva horsewoman when she grows up."

Laurie nearly fell off the fence. She'd been so lost in her thoughts that she hadn't heard Jake approach. He looked like the consummate cowboy, wearing his boots and his Stetson, a nylon horse's halter looped over his arm.

"Yes, I was just thinking that," Laurie said, trying not to sound as flustered as she felt. Why did he have to stand so close behind her? Why did he always have to look so sexy in those worn-to-white jeans of his that molded themselves so familiarly to his anatomy? Why did he have to smell so . . . so masculine?

"What about you?" he asked. "I've been here...what, three weeks? And I haven't seen you ride even once."

She sighed. "I haven't really had time..."

"You could make time, if you wanted to."

"Yes, I suppose I could." Actually, since she'd turned over the running of the Folly to Jake, she'd had to struggle to find activities to fill her days. "The truth is, I don't know which horse I'd ride," she said. "I've never ridden any but Flash."

"Oh, is that all? I know of one that would be perfect for you. That palomino—over there." He pointed to an adjoining pasture where several horses grazed on the verdant spring grass.

"You mean Magnolia? Right." Laurie laughed, thinking Jake must be joking. "She's not even broke."

"She doesn't need breaking. I've been working with her the past few days, getting her used to a saddle and bridle. This morning I jumped onto her back and she didn't do anything. She's calm as warm milk. And when I took her around the pasture, she handled like a dream. You'll love riding her."

"You aren't going to breed her this year?"

"No. I want to train her to be a barrel racer. She's got champion qualities stamped all over her. After she's made her mark on the rodeo circuit, then we'll breed her and make a fortune off her foals."

The way he was talking—as if he'd adopted the Folly's future as his own dream—made her uncomfortable. Training a horse to be a champion rodeo performer would take years. Did he really plan to be around that long?

"I don't barrel race, you know," she said.

"Ah, nothing to it," he said, dismissing her objections. "I was getting ready to bring—Magnolia, did you say?—into the barn, anyway. Ferrier's coming this afternoon to shoe the pony, and I thought I'd get Magnolia done, too. Why don't you come with me and help me catch her?"

"I'm supposed to be watching Wendy's lesson—"

"She'll never miss you."

Unfortunately Jake was right. Wendy wasn't paying the slightest bit of attention to her mother. She was totally focused on June Bug and Maurice's riding instructions.

Laurie had to admit she was intrigued with the idea of finding a new mount for herself. Pretty soon Wendy would be ready to leave the corral and ride around on the horse trails that crisscrossed the Folly, and Laurie would want to go with her. But she wasn't sure about Magnolia, and she was less sure about barrel racing.

Jake opened the gate to the pasture where four mares, including Magnolia, were grazing. When he whistled through his teeth, four heads raised up, and the horses immediately started loping toward Jake and Laurie.

It amazed Laurie that the darn horses would come to Jake like dogs. In the short time he'd been here, most of them had realized that Jake carried a never-ending supply of carrots with him at all times. He pulled two carrot pieces from his jeans and two more from his shirt pocket and fed them to the eager mares, who pushed and jostled one another. Casually Jake slipped the halter over Magnolia's head. The other horses, realizing the treats were gone, ambled away.

Laurie scratched the palomino's neck. "Hey, Maggie, how ya doing?" She turned to Jake. "She is a gorgeous animal. Of course, she would be. She's Flash's granddaughter.''

"And she definitely inherited her grandsire's temperament. Completely unflappable. Why don't you hop aboard?''

"What?" She laughed again, then looked down at her shorts and tennis shoes. "Jake, I'm hardly dressed for riding, and neither is Maggie.''

"Haven't you ever ridden bareback before?''

"Actually, no.''

"Then now's a good time to try it." Still holding on securely to Magnolia's halter, he leaned over and cupped his other hand next to the horse's ribs. "I'll give you a leg up." When Laurie still hesitated, he added, "Don't you trust me? You know I'd never ask you to do anything that was dangerous.''

Laurie had to agree. Reluctantly she stepped in front of him, grabbed on to the horse's mane and let him give her a boost onto the horse's back.

Magnolia turned her head to look curiously at Laurie, but that was the extent of her reaction.

Laurie had never imagined a horse's back to feel so soft and warm. As Jake led the mare slowly around the pasture, Laurie clung to her mane and gripped with her knees, feeling the powerful movement of equine muscle against her thighs. Within a short time she decided she liked bareback riding. She felt more connected to her mount than she had sitting on a big western saddle. This was definitely a more sensual experience.

When Magnolia suddenly stopped and tensed every muscle in her body, Laurie felt it immediately. "Jake?" That was all she managed to say before all hell broke loose. The horse snorted, gave a panicked whinny and reared up on her hind legs, pawing at the air.

"Whoa, whoa, girl," Jake said in a soothing voice.

Laurie tried her best to hold on, but she found herself sliding off the back of the horse. And Jake was there to catch her.

She grabbed on to him for dear life, her arms around his neck, her body sliding down his. "Oh—oh, my—"

"Easy, now," Jake said, and she wasn't sure if he was talking to her or the horse. With one arm around Laurie, he managed to catch hold of Magnolia's halter again with his free hand.

"You told me she wouldn't—"

"Quiet," Jake commanded. "Look."

Laurie followed Jake's gaze. A snake was coiled up not three feet in front of Magnolia, who was still pawing and snorting. No wonder the horse had gone wild.

"Is it poisonous?" Laurie whispered, still holding on to Jake. She couldn't seem to make herself let go.

"Hell, yeah, it's a copperhead."

"Can you kill it?"

"With what, my bare hands? No, we're just going to ease back from this standoff." As he spoke, he pulled on Magnolia's halter. The horse pranced and danced sideways, and Laurie held her breath as she waited for the snake to strike. But eventually Jake got the mare to back up. The snake, losing interest, turned and slithered away into some tall grass.

Laurie released a long pent-up breath. The danger had passed, but her body, plastered against Jake's, was still full of adrenaline.

Jake's attention, however, was on the horse, a fact that did little for Laurie's ego. "Good girl, Maggie. You did just fine."

Laurie forced herself to let go of Jake and step back, although she instinctively looked around for snakes first.

"Good girl?" she huffed. "She threw me. But I guess she did have a reason to panic. Can a copperhead kill a horse?"

"A bite can sure as hell make one go lame. But I'm more concerned about the fact that the snake could have bitten one of us. Or Wendy."

Laurie shivered at the thought.

"At least I'm wearing boots," Jake said. "Where are yours?"

"I didn't know I was going to be tromping around a snake-infested pasture when I dressed this morning." She bit her lower lip. Although poisonous snakes weren't a big problem on the ranch, Laurie knew there were a few. Charlie had always made a big deal about her wearing her boots, but frankly she hadn't thought about it in a while.

Wendy didn't even own a pair of boots.

The way Jake was looking at her, all burning intensity, she expected to get some kind of lecture. Then she realized he wasn't angry with her, but unnerved by the danger they'd narrowly avoided. He released the horse and grasped Laurie gently by the shoulders. "You sure you're okay?"

"Of course I'm okay. You broke my fall very nicely, thank you." She smiled, but he didn't smile back.

"I shouldn't have dragged you out here wearing tennis shoes."

"I'm the one who should have known better—"

"I can't stand the thought of anything happening to you." He gripped her shoulders more tightly. "I'd die if I caused you to get hurt falling off a horse, or to get bitten by a snake."

She'd never heard Jake say such a thing. Even when they were engaged, during their most passionate moments, she'd never pulled more than a reluctantly murmured, "Love you," out of him. She realized then that Jake really had changed. He was actually capable of revealing his feelings to her, putting them into words.

On the heels of that thought came the realization that he'd just admitted that he cared for her. Even more stunning was the fact that she could sense within herself a strong desire to reciprocate. Her immature love for him, which she'd thought long dead, had revived and ripened into something richer, something deeper.

She got scared then, and tried to pull away, but he held her fast.

"And I'm sorry I sold Flash. I did it partly because I wanted to hurt you. Afterward, I realized that wasn't what I wanted at all, and certainly not what you deserved. You can't be blamed for wanting to build a new life for yourself after I deserted you."

Laurie just stared, her mouth hanging open. Was she dreaming this? Was she standing in the middle of a pasture listening to Jake Mercer pour his heart out to her?

I only married Charlie because I was pregnant with your child. She almost told Jake, but she stopped herself in time. For the first time in his life Jake was opening up to her, telling her his feelings—telling her that she'd hurt him. They were at a delicate crossroads. What she said and did in the next few minutes might determine their whole future.

Oh, Lord, she was actually thinking in terms of a future. She was crazy, absolutely crazy.

Jake continued to look at her, waiting for some response.

"Charlie was a good man," she said carefully, "and a dedicated father and husband. But I didn't love him. Not the way I loved you."

Six

The way I loved you.

Loved. Past tense. Ah, hell, what did he expect? Jake wondered. Why was he standing out here spilling his guts, anyway? He'd planned to take things slowly, one step at a time, making sure he didn't ask for more than he really wanted, or more than Laurie was ready to give.

Seeing that snake, and watching Laurie tumble off that horse, had given him a turn. His mind had teemed with all the things that might have happened, all the things that could happen in the future. He'd panicked, he supposed.

But years ago, as he'd lain on that clammy, bug-infested pallet in Costa Rica, he'd prayed for the chance to survive his imprisonment and tell Laurie how he really felt about her. He'd bargained with God, promising that if he were allowed to live, he would never let pride prevent him from speaking his feelings.

But he hadn't planned on keeping his promise in exactly this fashion.

"If you didn't love him," Jake asked, "why did you marry him?"

"Most folks would say I was on the rebound," she replied in a carefully neutral voice. "They'd say I was primed and ready to be married and I grabbed at the first opportunity."

"And what do you say?"

She sighed. "I married Charlie for a lot of complicated and intensely personal reasons. And if you're really interested, I'll tell you about them."

Jake could tell she was uncomfortable. He didn't want to pry those personal things from her; he wanted her to tell him when she was ready.

He released his hold on her shoulders. "Someday I'd like for you to tell me," he said. But not now. He wasn't sure he really wanted, or needed, to know. It was enough that she'd admitted she hadn't loved Charlie. He would hold that bit of news to his heart and savor it for a while.

Magnolia was calmly grazing, having apparently forgotten her ordeal with the snake. Jake walked over to her and snagged her by the halter. "Come on, girl, let's go."

"Can we do anything about the snake?" Laurie asked.

"I'll move the other three horses to a different pasture, for now. Sometime this week Maurice and I'll clean out the brush and tall grass where snakes like to hide." He didn't add that he'd seen overgrown areas all over the Folly, which used to feature endless pastures of smooth, green Bermuda grass. It would again, if he had anything to say about it.

If Laurie would keep him around long enough to see it happen.

* * *

Laurie gazed out the kitchen window, one of her favorite spots these days. From this vantage point she could see the freshly painted barn, the greening pastures dotted with grazing horses and the flower garden she and Wendy had planted. The Folly was starting to look like its old self again, at least cosmetically.

As manager, Jake hadn't really done anything Laurie herself couldn't have done. But he'd taken steps she'd been afraid to take, making decisions with the confidence she'd lacked. He hadn't spun cash out of thin air, but sometimes it almost seemed as if he did. The money from Flash in the Pan's sale certainly had come in handy.

Jake himself was in the corral, exercising one of the horses on a lead rope. Laurie had to admit he was the best part of the view. She never tired of watching him move, even if he was simply walking.

There had been no more kisses, no more impassioned speeches, between them. But she'd stopped trying to avoid him, and instead had made every effort to be useful to him. She'd done everything from helping him clear brush to painting to grooming the horses, and she'd even started riding Magnolia. Jake had set up some barrels in one of the pastures, and she and the horse were learning together how to navigate around them.

She found that she was actually enjoying Jake's company in a way she never had before. They were sharing responsibilities as adults. He actually asked for her opinions, and she willingly sought his advice. It was a far cry from the relationship they'd had five years ago, in which Jake had always been the one in control.

Her woman's desire for him had changed, too, having sharpened and matured. They were both cautious on that level, but Laurie knew her willpower was growing thin, and she suspected Jake's was, too. The prospect of making love to him was not as frightening and disastrous-seeming as it had been a few weeks ago. She was actually beginning to think it was inevitable, and that perhaps she ought to look forward to it.

Jake pulled his hat off and wiped his brow with the back of his hand, and she sighed. Lord, he was gorgeous.

Go make yourself useful instead of daydreaming, she scolded herself. But with Wendy gone to the Grand Canyon with her grandparents, there was precious little to keep Laurie busy.

She was about to decide to take Magnolia out for a ride when a car pulled into the driveway, a big brown sedan. Laurie didn't recognize the car, so she watched from the window to see who got out.

The man in his forties with thinning blond hair looked familiar, but she couldn't quite place him. He'd parked his car by the corral fence and was heading straight toward Jake, so it was probably nothing she needed to concern herself with. Still, she watched. Was he an old friend of Jake's? Someone wanting to buy or sell a horse, perhaps?

Jake dropped the horse's lead rope and walked up to the fence, awkwardly shaking hands with the man through the rails. Then he folded his arms in a stance that was clearly confrontational. Although his hat shadowed his face, Laurie got the distinct impression Jake was scowling.

Now her curiosity was really piqued. She was seeing a bit of the Jake she remembered, the intense, aggressive man who got his way come hell or high water. She decided she needed to meet this visitor, whoever he was, and find out why he'd gotten Jake's back up.

She quickly changed into jeans and boots—which she'd worn religiously ever since the snake incident—and headed outdoors.

She decided to satisfy her curiosity head-on. With a smile and a wave, which Jake barely acknowledged, she brazenly strode right up to the two men. "Hi, I'm Laurie Birkett," she said to the stranger, extending her hand.

"Tom Cesore," he said, hastily shaking her hand and flashing a brief, distant smile.

Conversation screeched to a dead halt. Neither man offered any further explanation as to why Mr. Cesore had come, or what business he had with Jake. Whatever they'd been discussing so intensely was apparently not for her ears.

"Well, uh, nice to meet you, Mr. Cesore," she said. "I'm off for a ride."

"I put Magnolia in the barn for you," Jake replied. "She seems eager for some, uh, attention."

And you seem eager to be rid of me, Laurie thought with a scowl of her own as she headed for the barn.

She found the little palomino mare waiting for her in a stall—except it was difficult to tell she was a palomino, because her coat was covered with dried mud. Now Laurie knew what Jake meant when he'd said the horse needed "attention."

"Oh, Maggie, just look at you," Laurie said as she found a currycomb. "You'd think you were a pig instead of a horse, the way you like to roll in mud." As she energetically curried the animal, her thoughts drifted back to Tom Cesore. And then she remembered where she'd seen him before, and she almost cried out in her alarm.

Cesore was Jake's boss in the Marshals Service. Former boss, Laurie reminded herself. Jake was out of law enforcement now, and he had no intention of returning to it. At least, he'd told her that, and she'd believed him.

Then what was Cesore doing here? If it was strictly a social call, they wouldn't have clammed up when she'd approached. What if Jake's old boss was trying to hire him back? Jake would be crazy not to at least consider it. The Marshals Service offered more excitement, better hours and better pay than a grueling job on a struggling ranch.

A sob bubbled up from somewhere deep inside her, and it took her a few moments to realize the source of her distress. She was truly upset at the thought of Jake leaving the Folly. A few weeks ago she'd been dead set against his coming here, and now she couldn't imagine looking out her kitchen window and not seeing him hard at work.

Even more distressing was the idea of his returning to the Marshals Service, putting his life on the line every day. His role in law enforcement hadn't bothered her before, when they were engaged. She'd been proud to be marrying such an upstanding sort of guy, and the possibility of his being injured or killed had seemed fuzzy, dreamlike, and extremely remote.

Things were different now—now that she'd lost him once to a bullet.

She tried to swallow back a second sob, but it pushed past her throat and erupted noisily. Before she knew it she had her face pressed against Magnolia's neck, crying into her mane. The harder she tried to stop, the more tears gushed forth.

This was ridiculous! There was no reason to fall apart just because Jake's old boss had stopped by. He could be here for a million reasons besides trying to recruit Jake.

When she heard footsteps—Jake's footsteps, she was sure—on the packed dirt floor, she tried desperately to compose herself. Turning her back toward the stall door, she renewed her efforts at cleaning Maggie's muddy coat, hoping Jake would pass right on by her.

No such luck.

"I meant to warn you about Maggie's disreputable state. I found her this morning rolling in the mud at the edge of the tank. She was real pleased with herself, too. You want a hand cleaning her up?"

Laurie sniffed loudly. "Uh, no thanks."

"Laurie?" he said sharply. "What's wrong?"

She brushed all the more vigorously. "Nothing."

"The hell it's nothing. You're crying."

"Am not. Now go away."

Paying no attention to her order, he opened the stall door, came up behind her and gently swiveled her around to face him. She couldn't very well disguise her damp cheeks, so she looked up at him defiantly. She wanted to tell him to leave her alone, that if she wanted to cry it was her business. But the concern she saw in his blue eyes made it impossible to even pretend anger.

"Laurie, what is it? Are you missing Wendy?" She didn't answer. "Did Magnolia step on your foot?" When she remained silent, he sighed deeply. "Don't make me play twenty questions."

"Why was Tom Cesore here to see you?" she asked, failing to hide her utter contempt for the man.

Jake seemed taken aback by the question. "He just wanted to talk about some old business. Nothing that should concern you."

"Of course it concerns me! If he talks you into returning to the Marshals Service, I'll be left without a manager."

"Is that why you're crying? You think I'm gonna quit?"

"Is that what he came here for?" she persisted, determined that Jake would answer her question before she answered his.

"He mentioned that there's an opening, but—"

"I knew it! He came here to offer you your old job back. Are you going to take it?" She held her breath, expecting the worst.

"If you would let me finish...I told him I wouldn't even consider going back to the Marshals Service. That chapter of my life was over years ago. I'm a ranch manager now, a horse breeder, and I like that just fine."

Moisture pooled in Laurie's eyes again, but these were tears of relief. "I'm...glad," she managed in a choked voice, turning away to swipe at the tears with the back of her hand. She was mortified to do this in front of Jake, but she was so unutterably relieved she wasn't going to lose him that she didn't care.

"Laurie, what is the problem? If you don't tell me why you're crying I'm going to tickle you until you tell me."

His threat, one she remembered from childhood, made her laugh despite herself. It seemed perfectly natural for her to slip her arms under his and give him a great big hug. "It doesn't matter why I was crying before. I'm fine now."

He hesitated only a moment before returning the hug, holding her head against his shoulder and rubbing her back. "Is this one of those hormonal things?"

She would have punched him in the ribs, but he sounded so genuinely bewildered by her behavior that she couldn't. "I was crying because I was afraid you were going to leave, okay? I was afraid you were going to go back to the Marshals Service and get yourself shot again.''

Jake was silent for a long time, though he continued to massage her back and run his fingers through her hair. ''You were crying over me,'' he finally said.

''You don't have to rub it in,'' Laurie said, her voice muffled against his shirt. ''I can't help it if I'm an idiot.''

He pressed his cheek against the top of her head. ''I'm not going anywhere, Laurie. I'm here for as long as you'll have me. I can admit now that one of the reasons I offered to work on the Folly was so I'd have an excuse to be near you again. But I'm really enjoying the work. I think this was what I was meant to do. In fact, I think I could do this the rest of my life.''

Laurie was afraid to look up at him, but she did, anyway, and what she saw took her breath away. He gazed down on her with such undisguised hope, and she realized that just now he had, in his own way, renewed his commitment to her—not just to the ranch, but to her personally.

Through a film of tears she smiled back, knowing full well she was saying yes to his unasked question. Slowly he lowered his head and kissed her with infinite tenderness, a kiss that spoke not just volumes but whole libraries about how he cared for her.

Laurie's heart was so full it felt as if it might explode. Everything she'd ever hoped for glittered invitingly, a bright beacon toward the future. She pulled herself more tightly against Jake and kissed him back as the passion she'd banked for so long escaped its walls and swamped her whole body. She met his tongue with hers, tasting, filling herself with the essence of him.

A warm, soft horse's nose pushed at Laurie's elbow. When she ignored it, it tried to snuffle Jake's ear, then knocked his hat off.

"Ach!" Jake objected as he abruptly ended the kiss.

"Hey, get your own guy," Laurie said, laughing at the mare's bid for attention. Jake still held Laurie in a loose embrace, and she leaned her head against his shoulder. "You know, that's what we get for kissing in a barn."

"Maybe we should try kissing someplace else."

"Like?"

When he answered, his voice was so husky it was almost a whisper. "My bedroom."

Laurie's blood warmed as memories of their single night of lovemaking flooded her mind. For so long she'd clung to those images, tried to keep them from fading. Suddenly she wanted him with a sharpness that took her breath away. She wanted to again experience his tenderness, his fierce passion. She wanted to feel her body awaken to his touch, to have him rediscover the physical responses that were still mysterious even to her.

He leaned down to graze another soft kiss against her lips. "Your decision, honey. Like I said before, I don't see any reason to delay when it comes to romance, but I've learned to be a patient man. I know you'll come to me when you're ready."

Patience didn't appear to be in her vocabulary at the moment. She was tingling all over, her body aching for Jake's touch. She remembered how badly she'd wanted him once, and how she'd convinced herself she should wait ... and wait. And for what? A single, thin slice of heaven that was brutally smashed to bits the following day.

"I'm ready," she said. "But Maurice—"

"Is in Navasota at an auction, remember? Won't be back till tomorrow." Jake took the currycomb from Laurie's limp hand and set it aside. Then he swung her up in his arms, kicked the stall door open and carried her through it.

She laughed at his antics. "You're going to carry me all the way to your house?"

"It'll be my pleasure." He nudged the stall door closed with his elbow and proceeded to deliver his promise.

The short trip to Jake's cottage gave Laurie just enough time for her logical mind to come up with a few objections. "Jake, are we doing the right thing?" she asked as he gently set her down in the small but neat living room.

He brought her hand to his lips and brushed an absent kiss against her knuckles, causing her a pleasurable shiver. "I'm not sure I even know what the right thing or the wrong thing is anymore. I think all we can do is make a stab at something, and then find out later whether we made the right decision."

She wanted to believe him. On the eve of her wedding when she and Jake had made love the first time, if she had known what would happen later would she still have done it? Perhaps not. And yet, if they'd denied themselves that pleasure, she wouldn't have Wendy.

Laurie uncurled her hand from around his and caressed his lean face, then ran her fingers through his black hair, fluffing it out where his hat had mashed it down. "In that case, can I take a shower?"

"What?" He stared at her incredulously.

"I smell like horses."

He smiled indulgently, then leaned down and kissed her neck. "You smell great to me. Kinda outdoorsy."

"But, Jake..."

"We'll compromise. You can wash your hands." Grasping her around her waist he propelled her toward the kitchenette. As she stood at the sink lathering her hands and forearms, and he stood behind her, his warm breath ruffling her hair, she decided a shower had been a dumb idea. They were both strung so tightly they were in danger of falling on top of each other right here on the kitchen floor if they didn't find a bed—and soon.

Jake reached around her, took the bar of soap and began lathering up his own hands. Then he took her hands in his, rubbing her palms and her fingers, her wrists and her sensitive inner arm, the soap bubbles sliding sensually between their skins.

"Hmm, maybe I shouldn't have ruled out the shower, after all," he said, pushing suggestively against her bottom.

She sagged against the edge of the sink, her eyes closed, her breathing coming in small, rapid gasps. That kitchen floor was looking better all the time.

Jake turned the faucet until the stream of water was warm, then washed the soap away. He didn't even bother with a towel. He put his wet hands on her shoulder, soaking her cotton blouse, and turned her around to face him. "You have no idea what you do to me."

"Oh, yes, I do," she assured him, throwing her dripping hands around his neck and pressing a wanton kiss to his waiting mouth.

The tenderness he'd shown earlier had vanished, replaced with raw need. Her caution disappeared, and in its place was a rapacious hunger that had gnawed at her belly for years. When Jake placed his hands on her bottom and hitched her up, she wrapped her legs around his lean hips and he carried her that way, still kissing her, into the bedroom.

The lonely years that had lain between them melted away. Laurie felt like a young girl again, unburdened by the harsh realities of life, as Jake fumbled in his haste to unbutton her blouse. The intimacies they'd shared for months before the wedding—the kissing and touching, bringing each other to the brink of satisfaction, the almost-but-not-quite making love—came back to her in a barrage of heated memories. There was no awkwardness, no relearning of each other's bodies.

It was, miraculously, as if they'd never been apart.

She removed Jake's shirt, reveling in the remembered feel of his bare chest, the coarse hair that tickled her palms, the well-defined muscles that quivered at her touch.

But some things had changed, she admitted. She was not as timid as she'd been back then. And Jake wasn't as ill prepared. He turned away from her momentarily to rummage around in his dresser, finally coming up with a square plastic package, which he showed to her with all the panache of a wine steward asking for approval on a bottle of burgundy.

She nodded, realizing that birth control hadn't even occurred to her—just like last time. That was all she needed, to conceive another child out of wedlock with Jake Mercer. Grateful for his protecting her, impulsively she laid her cheek against his chest, then kissed his flat brown nipple.

He moaned. "Laurie..."

"Do you want me to stop?"

"No, I—hell, you're making me crazy. Where did you—"

He stopped himself, but Laurie knew what he'd been about to say: Where did you learn that?

The years that had separated them intruded again, briefly. She couldn't pretend that she hadn't had sex with her husband, and she wasn't the same inexperienced virgin she'd been the last time she and Jake were together. But this wasn't the time to think about that, and thank goodness Jake realized that, too.

He explored her bare back with questing hands, pausing to caress her bottom through the denim of her jeans. "Too many clothes," he murmured. "Can we do something about that?"

Laurie didn't need to be asked twice. Although having Jake undress her was beautiful in her fantasies, the reality of pulling off boots and tight jeans was something else again. She quickly kicked off the boots and shucked the jeans as Jake did the same until they were both standing there in their underwear.

She heard Jake suck in his breath. "Let me do the rest, honey," he said as he stepped unselfconsciously out of his teal blue briefs.

She nodded numbly, frankly awed by the sight of Jake's nude body. She realized with a start that she had never seen him that way. Their times together before had always consisted of hasty, guilty intimacies in the dark. The one time they'd made love it had been late at night, and they'd both been a little tipsy from the wine served at the rehearsal dinner.

He was utterly perfect, better than any fantasy—wide shouldered, slim hipped, flat bellied. She couldn't help remembering that Charlie had been barrel chested and thin limbed, but sinewy. "All gristle," he'd joked. She silently apologized to both men for allowing the intrusive thought to take hold. Charlie would forgive her unflattering comparison, but Jake wouldn't appreciate her thoughts touching even briefly on any man but him.

When Jake cupped her lace-covered breasts in his big hands, all thoughts of anything but him vanished. He made a ritual out of removing her bra, kissing the tender flesh between her breasts as he unfastened the front clasp, sliding the straps slowly down her arms, his gaze fastened on the pale, rose-tipped treasures he had just uncovered.

For a split second she was aware of the fact that she no longer had the lithe girl's body Jake would remember. Pregnancy had left her with several additional pounds and the curves she'd longed for in adolescence, not to mention a few stretch marks.

If Jake noticed, he didn't care. He ran his fingertips up and down her midriff, and the light in his eyes told her he liked what he saw and felt. He slid his hands inside her flowered nylon panties, pausing a moment to simply caress her bottom before slowly lowering the wispy garment down her legs.

As he leaned down, she caught sight of the ugly scar on his back where the bullet had torn his flesh. So near the spine, she thought, reaching out involuntarily to touch the puckered skin.

"I ain't as pretty as I used to be," he drawled.

"I'm not as skinny as I used to be," she returned.

"Yeah, but I like those curves. I'll have to drive real slow-like to make sure I don't skid right off the highway." She started to laugh, but when he kissed her belly and circled her navel with his tongue, the laugh caught in her throat.

Her knees went weak and she sank onto the haphazardly made bed, kicking her underwear aside. Jake fell beside her and gathered her against him, and for a moment she simply savored the feel of his hard body against hers, his hot arousal pulsating against her thigh.

By silent agreement they moved to the center of the bed. Then Jake proceeded to explore her every hill and valley from her scalp to the soles of her feet—"driving slowly," just as he'd promised. He kissed and caressed, teased and tickled, until she was in a frenzy, completely out of her head with wanting him.

"Oh, Jake, I want you," she said, hearing a plaintiveness in her voice that surprised her.

Maybe that was what he'd been waiting for, because he immediately found that little plastic packet where it had fallen on the bed and ripped it open with his teeth. Properly sheathed, he covered her body with his and she eagerly parted her legs for him. He poised himself briefly at her opening, a questioning look on his face. At her almost imperceptible nod, he slipped inside her, filling her, completing her. And for the next few minutes she reclaimed that small slice of heaven that had been so cruelly taken away.

Their coupling was fast and almost brutal in its intensity, but Laurie didn't care. She cried out with total abandon when she climaxed, and moments later he did the same. Then they simply lay together, panting, slick with perspiration. As the passion-fog cleared from Laurie's mind, allowing her to see beyond the immediate satisfaction of physical needs, she wondered for the first time what would come next.

Seven

"Now that's the way every working man should spend his afternoons," Jake said when his breathing slowed enough that he could talk again.

Laurie remained silent, a pensive look on her face.

"What, no comment, boss lady?" He stroked her velvet cheek with his knuckles, and she clasped his hand and held it against her face.

"Was it like you remembered?" she asked suddenly.

"Better," he answered without hesitation. "Better than my memories, better than my fantasies. You know, sometimes, when I was in Costa Rica, thoughts of you were all that kept me alive. I used to imagine all the things I would do to you—with you—when I got free and came back to Winnefred."

"And then I spoiled your plans by being married when you finally did come back. I'm sorry for that, Jake. I'm sorry for hurting you."

"You didn't hurt me," he said gruffly, lying through his teeth. "Just surprised me a little."

The afternoon had grown warm. Jake got up and turned on the old ceiling fan above them, then returned to bed. He flopped onto his stomach, scrunched one of the pillows against his neck and threw a possessive arm across Laurie's middle. "Was it like you remembered?" he asked.

"No. I mean, at times I could almost forget about all the years and the events that came between us. But it seemed like every few seconds, something would remind me that we aren't the same two people who made love on the eve of their wedding. Things were so simple then, so black-and-white."

"Are things so complicated now?" he asked.

She closed her eyes. "Yes."

He'd been afraid of that. "Does that mean that you're going to tell me this was a terrible mistake and we have to forget it happened?"

She turned onto her side, facing him, and slipped one arm under her pillow, mirroring his pose. He got the distinct impression she was rearranging her thoughts as she rearranged her body.

"No, Jake," she finally said. "I couldn't forget making love with you any more than I could forget my name. All I'm saying is that we can't go back. We aren't the same two people we were five years ago. We've changed, the world has changed, and if we want to... have a... a relationship, we really need to start all over and do it on completely different terms than we did before."

"What terms?"

"I don't know. We make them up as we go along, I guess. All I know is we can't expect to have what we had before, and it would be silly to try and recapture those feelings. What we had before is lost forever.''

''And who's to say we can't build something even better, hmm?'' He ran his hand down her side and across her hip.

Her eyes widened briefly, then half closed as she sighed helplessly. ''I want more than sex between us,'' she said.

''So do I. But this isn't a bad place to start, right?''

''Mmm.''

He smiled and leaned over to give her a playful kiss, but Laurie's response was decidedly more than playful. She grabbed on to his shoulders and held him close, raising her head off the pillow and kissing him back with enough steam to press the sheets.

''Uh, Laurie,'' he said, breaking the kiss. ''Didn't you just point out that I'm not the same man as five years ago? I'm also not quite as young, and if you want—oh.''

Smiling wickedly, she'd boldly caressed him in a way she would have found unthinkable years earlier, reviving his desire more swiftly than he would have believed possible. She batted her lashes. ''You were saying?''

''I was going to say that no matter how old I am, you make me feel like a hormone-crazed eighteen-year-old.''

''Good.''

''And it's gonna get better.''

Laurie sprawled on the rumpled sheets, letting the breeze from the ceiling fan dry her sweat-sheened body, letting its rhythmic rattling lull her into a state of half sleep.

She hadn't felt this peaceful in...well, she didn't know when. She'd had her doubts about the wisdom of going to bed with Jake. But afterward, when she'd talked to him, he'd seemed to understand perfectly even though she hadn't voiced her concerns very eloquently.

He'd said and done all the right things. He'd reassured her that he was interested in more than sex with her, yet he hadn't pushed her to put a name to her expectations—which was good, since she wasn't sure exactly what she expected.

A relationship. She knew she wanted that. But she had no intention of rushing into some kind of commitment just because they'd shared a bed. She wasn't going to brainwash herself into believing Jake was some paragon of husbandly virtues simply because he'd made love to her in the most perfect way she could imagine. But she was going to keep her mind open to all possibilities, and it sounded as if Jake wanted to do the same.

It seemed too good to be true.

It was too good to be true. She'd forgotten one not-so-minor detail—Wendy. She had to tell Jake, and she had to tell him now, even at the risk of destroying the fragile trust that had begun to build between them. It was going to be painful, perhaps even heartbreaking, but farther down the road it would be much, much worse.

She could do it, she coached herself. She now trusted Jake to handle the news well. She was hopeful that he would understand why she'd waited to tell him, and to honor her wishes to keep the matter private.

"Jake?"

"Mmm?" His face was against the pillow, his voice muffled.

Just as well. She was afraid to see his expression when she told him. "There's something we need to discuss, and I hope you'll forgive me for waiting this long. But I've had to sort some things out in my mind, get my priorities straight."

She paused, waiting for a reaction. When Jake said nothing, she took a deep breath and continued. "My biggest concern is for Wendy. I can't do anything that would harm her. Or Charlie. I owe such a debt to Charlie, it can't ever be repaid. He gave me a home and security, and he gave . . . he gave my baby a name. He was the most devoted father you can imagine. Jake, do you get what I'm saying?"

His silence terrified her.

"Wendy is your child," she said, just to make sure there was no question. And when he still said nothing she looked down at him . . . and saw that his eyes were closed, his jaw relaxed. "Jake?"

He snored softly.

"Oh, for God's sake," she said in disgust as the knot in her stomach relaxed. All that angst for nothing. The clod was asleep.

She smiled fondly and ruffled his midnight hair, then snuggled down closer to him and succumbed to the lazy spring afternoon. First thing when they woke up, she promised herself. First thing.

Sometime later Laurie was abruptly awakened by a shouted, "No!" She bolted upright in bed, fists clenched, ready to take on any enemy . . . until she realized Jake was the one crying out, and he was still asleep.

He tossed his head back and forth and threw his hands out in front of him, as if warding off an assault. "No, no," he said on a moan. His legs thrashed about in the tangled bed covers.

Laurie was paralyzed with indecision. She'd always heard that you shouldn't wake up someone in the midst of a nightmare, but she couldn't stand to see Jake so tortured. Abruptly she made her choice, grasping his shoulders and shaking. "Jake, wake up!"

He flung out one arm at his unseen enemy and clipped her on the mouth, hard enough that she tasted blood.

"Ow! Dammit, Jake." She grabbed both of his hands in hers to keep them from flailing. "Jake! Wake up!"

His eyes flew open. It took a few seconds, but recognition dawned in their blue depths and they focused on her. His arms relaxed. "Laurie?"

"That must have been some nightmare." Her heart was pounding, her body jumping with adrenaline.

Jake sat up, looked at her again, then ran the tip of his thumb along her swollen lip. "Did I do that?"

She nodded. "'Fraid so, slugger."

"Oh, Laurie." He put his arms around her as gently as if she were made of spun glass. "I'm so sorry, honey."

"It's okay. You didn't know it was me you were punching at. Who were you trying to hit? I mean, what in the world were you dreaming about?"

He paused the length of a heartbeat before answering. "I don't remember."

She could tell he was lying, that he wanted to shield her from his nightmares. "Does this have anything to do with Costa Rica?" They'd been talking about that earlier.

It was as if someone had pulled window shades down on Jake's eyes. They were still open, still looking at her, but he had closed off his mind to her. "I don't want to think about that right now." He brushed his mouth against hers. "Let me get some ice for that busted lip."

Jake pulled on his jeans and left Laurie alone in the bedroom. She tried to summon the necessary energy to get dressed, but she only got as far as her bra and panties before she dropped back onto the bed, lost in thought.

Had he been tortured in Costa Rica? She'd never given much thought to what he'd gone through during those months of captivity. She hadn't wanted to think about it. She didn't want to think about it now. But she had to. His body had healed, but she couldn't be too sure about the rest of him until he confided in her.

Well, time enough for that, she thought pragmatically. Getting to know Jake again, allowing him to know her, wouldn't be an overnight process.

He returned with a couple of ice cubes wrapped in a clean dishcloth and handed them to her. "Hold that on your mouth for a while," he said as he donned his shirt. "I'll go feed the horses."

"I'll help," she said, mumbling around the makeshift ice pack, suddenly aware of her state of undress. She looked around for the rest of her clothes.

"I don't need help," he said. "Stay here awhile, relax."

"I have to start dinner soon."

"We'll go out to dinner. Um, let me rephrase that. Can I take you out to dinner, Laurie?"

She had to smile. The old Jake wouldn't have thought to ask. "I would enjoy that very much. But somewhere out of Winnefred, okay?"

"You afraid of the gossip? You know tongues have been wagging since the day I got here. The rumor mill has had us sleeping together, secretly married and divorced ten times over at least."

Laurie had suspected that, but at least the townspeople had enough manners not to repeat the gossip to her face. "I'd just rather not spend the whole evening explaining a fat lip."

"Good point," he said as he buckled his belt. "We'll drive to Tyler."

As she heard the front door slam, she realized she'd passed up another opportunity to tell Jake about Wendy.

Jake heaved two bales of alfalfa from the truck into the feed trough at the largest pasture, where most of the Folly's horses spent their spring days. He felt good—better than he had in years. He and Laurie had made a start at building something solid, something that would last.

He'd hoped it would come to this eventually, but he'd never dreamed it would happen so quickly. He'd expected Laurie to regret their impulsive lovemaking, and that he would have to spend considerable energy convincing her they hadn't made a mistake.

But she was handling their decision like the mature woman she'd grown into. She hadn't immediately declared her undying love or expressed any interest in marriage, but she had used the dreaded *R* word—Relationship. That was a beginning.

Maybe he was the one who needed to slow down and act like a grown-up. Holding Laurie in his arms again had got him thinking about white picket fences and family photo albums, little brothers and sisters for Wendy, weekend trips to Galveston.

There was one small fly in the ointment, however. He hadn't told Laurie the whole truth about Tom Cesore. Yes, his former boss had mentioned an opening for a deputy marshal, and Jake had expressed no interest. But the main reason Tom had stopped by was to warn him. Rumors had surfaced that Juan LaBarba was back, and that he was bent on revenge against Jake for killing his brother.

Never mind that Jake hadn't actually pulled the trigger of the gun that had killed Ernesto LaBarba. Jake had become a convenient target for Juan's vengeance.

Jake had pretty much dismissed the rumor. He'd heard similar talk before, and it never panned out. But on some subconscious level he must have believed Tom. Why else would he have had the nightmare about Costa Rica?

He used to have them all the time, but they'd eventually tapered off. He hadn't had one in more than six months. He was sorry Laurie had witnessed it, and mortified that the violence of his past life had spilled on to her, even by accident. He wanted to shield her from ever knowing what the LaBarbas had done to him. The confinement, lack of exercise and sunlight, nonexistent medical care and rotten food had almost killed him.

But it was the psychological torture that had done the most damage. Embittered by the loss of his brother, Juan LaBarba had found Jake's weakest spot—Laurie—and taken full advantage. He would tell Jake that he had captured Laurie, tortured her, raped her, killed her. Jake had tried not to believe the stories, but part of him feared they were true, and that fear grew to overwhelming proportions until Jake was in danger of losing his sanity.

It was only when Carmen, Juan's wife, took pity on him and told him Juan was lying that Jake recovered enough wits to escape. Carmen had cared for him physically, too, putting poultices on his wound, giving him vile-tasting medicines to lower his fever. He hoped Juan never found out about Carmen's role in Jake's escape.

As Jake fed and watered the horses in the barn and the small front pasture, he consciously pushed thoughts of Costa Rica aside. Tonight he was taking Laurie on a date. He would pick some out-of-the-way place with soft music and candlelight, and they could fall in love all over again. Then he would bring her back here and . . .

His jeans grew uncomfortably tight, and he had to consciously shift his thoughts again. Oats. He needed to order more oats from the Feed Lot. And he'd been thinking about getting a new bridle for June Bug while Wendy was away. The old one was stretched and frayed.

When he finished the afternoon chores he went to the main house, where the ranch's office was maintained in an extra bedroom. On the way he passed Laurie's bathroom, heard the water running, heard her singing off key.

He smiled and resisted the urge to join her in the shower. He didn't want to crowd her when things between them were so new and fresh. He wasn't yet intimate enough with her to know her comfort zones—but he intended to find out. Whistling tunelessly, he continued on to the office.

Jake wasn't the kind of person who enjoyed office work, but he knew just enough about bookkeeping and business management to do a competent job. He couldn't fault Laurie's record keeping. She—and probably Charlie before her—had kept the accounts up-to-date and the filing neat and orderly. It had taken Jake only a few short hours to familiarize himself with the office and how everything worked.

He didn't intend to spend much time in there today, but he did want to call the Feed Lot and order some oats.

When he dialed the number, he got Danny Branson himself on the phone. "Hey, Danny, it's Jake. I need to order some feed, and I'll pick it up tomorrow."

"Hey, Jake. No problem. In fact, I can deliver it on my way home. I'm due for a visit with Laurie, anyway. Got some fence mending to do."

"She still mad at you for not telling her about me?"

"*Mad* isn't quite the word I would use. *Furious,* maybe? *Rabid* comes to mind."

Jake chuckled. "She'll get over it. But if you come by this evening, she won't be here."

"Oh? Where's she going?"

"Out to dinner. With me." Jake held his breath and waited for Danny's inevitable reaction. Although Danny had never disapproved of Jake in the same way his and Laurie's parents did, he'd never been all that wild about his best friend marrying his baby sister, either.

"You startin' things up with Laurie again?" Danny asked with deceptive casualness.

"I'm not sure what's happening," Jake replied honestly. "But I do know that, if we get back together, it'll be different this time. She'll be the most important thing in my life. She'll always come first."

"See that she does," Danny said in a not-so-subtle warning. But when he spoke again, his voice was once again friendly. "I'll deliver the feed, anyway, and leave it in the barn. It's on my way home. Watcha need?"

Jake told him, then quickly concluded the conversation. He reached for the Day-at-a-Glance calendar, intending to jot down a reminder about June Bug's bridle. With his mind so full of Laurie, he didn't trust himself to remember on his own.

He flipped ahead to the next day, but his pen froze above the page. There was already a notation there. The date was circled in red, and underneath it, in big red letters, was written, "Wendy's B.D."—in Laurie's handwriting.

Wendy's birthday? That didn't make sense, according to what he'd learned secondhand from Danny about Laurie's pregnancy. Wendy had been born in the fall, he thought. But what if . . .

Jake quickly did the math in his head, then did it again to be sure, then used the calculator. The conclusion was inescapable. Laurie hadn't been pregnant when Jake had come back from Costa Rica, as Danny had claimed. She'd already had the baby.

She'd been pregnant when she married Charlie. *Pregnant with my child.*

His chest swelled with joy and pride at the realization that he was a father, that he and Laurie had conceived a child on the eve of their wedding. Wendy was his flesh and blood. And Laurie hadn't fallen into another man's arms immediately after Jake's disappearance, as he'd believed. She'd married Charlie to give the baby a name.

On the heels of that seed of pure, blinding joy came other, more uncomfortable realizations. Another man had been there for Laurie during her pregnancy. Another man had first held that baby and felt the pride of fatherhood. Another man had fed her late-night bottles, changed her diaper, witnessed her first steps. Wendy called that man her daddy. She had a picture of him in her room.

Discomfort quickly changed to anger. Jake had been lied to, first by Danny, then by Laurie. And surely others knew—Maurice, whom he'd come to think of as a friend; Laurie's parents; even his own parents! And no one had bothered to tell him he had a child. Why?

Hell, it didn't matter why. The omission filled him with an unreasoning rage. He had a right to know. And especially now, when Wendy needed a father so badly, he had not only the right, but the obligation, to be that father.

What had Laurie been thinking, to keep something so precious from him?

He ripped the page out of the calendar and stormed out of the office, straight to Laurie's bathroom door. Without pausing to think what he would say to her, he pounded on the door with his fist.

"Just a minute," came her unconcerned voice from behind the door. "Goodness, you don't have to break the door down." She opened the door a crack, and a wisp of fragrant steam escaped. She peered out, her hair wet and tangled, her body wrapped in a pink towel, and for a split second Jake's anger faltered.

But he had only to think of Wendy, and the lie, and the fury bubbled up again, nearly choking him. He thrust the torn date book page at her. "You want to explain this?"

Laurie looked at the scrap of paper and her face drained of all color. "From the looks of things," she said, her voice shaky, "I don't have to explain it. You already know."

Eight

Laurie felt dizzy, and the steamy bathroom seemed suddenly hot and suffocating. Why now? Why did he have to discover the truth now, when she would have told him about Wendy at dinner?

She closed her eyes and bit her lip. Her best intentions didn't exonerate her. She should have told him long before now, instead of being such a coward. And when she peeked at Jake's face, she could see that he more than agreed with her.

"I was going to tell you..." she began lamely.

"When? At her college graduation?"

"Today, in fact," she continued, though she had a feeling nothing she could say would make Jake understand, or lessen his anger. "I tried to tell you earlier, when we were in.... Don't you remember, I said I had something to discuss with you? And I told you about Wendy, but you'd fallen asleep."

"How convenient for you."

"You think I'm lying?" She clutched at the door-frame to keep herself from falling.

"It wouldn't be the first time. If you were planning to tell me about Wendy, why did you send her on vacation with your parents over her birthday?"

"Because I wanted to decide how and when you were told," Laurie retorted, getting angry herself. Perhaps she'd made an error in judgment, but did that give Jake the right to interrogate her?

His face was as hard as granite. "You could have told me the first time Wendy grabbed on to my leg and called me Daddy. But you chose to keep me in the dark. You, and Danny and Maurice and the whole goddamn town, for all I know. Does everyone know, Laurie?"

She wished she could shield him from this part. But she had no choice now. She had to tell him everything. "Anyone who bothered to count the months knew, Jake. But they didn't tell you probably for the same reason that I hesitated to. Charlie was an exceptional father to my little girl, and no one wants to take that away from him."

She could tell that that particular truth hurt him most of all. He closed his eyes and pressed his lips together. "I would have been a good father. You know damn well I'd have been here for her, for you, if I could have been. I didn't abandon you. But you're acting like I did. You're punishing me for something I had no control over."

"I wasn't punishing you," she insisted, swallowing back the tears that threatened. "I did what I thought was best at the time. I know it's not fair to you, but you have to understand," she said desperately. "My first responsibility is to Wendy."

Jake closed his eyes and put his fingertips to his forehead. "I understand that. It would have been a tough decision to make, when you couldn't be sure why I was here, or whether I was going to stick around."

She felt some measure of relief. At least he was trying to see her side of it.

"But you know me well enough by now to have a little faith. You must realize I would never willingly abandon my own child."

"Yes, I do believe that."

He paused, his brow furrowed, obviously trying very hard to come to terms with her deception, trying to understand the reasons for it. She began to think this would all work out.

Then Jake asked, "When do we tell Wendy?"

"Oh, Jake, we can't tell her."

"What?"

"Charlie is the only father she's ever known. I've only recently gotten her to accept the fact that he's not coming back, that he's in heaven. If you come along claiming to be her father—"

"I am her father."

"I know, but..." How could she explain this? Jake hadn't been here to see Charlie's very special relationship with Wendy. Still, she tried. "Charlie accepted Wendy into his life as if she were his own flesh and blood. She was never a stepdaughter to him. They shared a bond. Charlie doesn't deserve to have that bond diminished or de-emphasized. In all the ways that are important, he was Wendy's father."

"And I'm nothing?" In a flash Jake's anger had returned, and if anything he seemed even more vehement than before. "I'm Wendy's father, and she damn well is going to know it."

Laurie felt panic closing in on her. Jake was beyond reason, and until he calmed down she wouldn't be able to woo him to her way of thinking. The only choice left to her was to take a hard stand. "Don't fight me on this, Jake. I know what's best for my little girl. And if you try to claim her, you won't get any support, not from me or Danny or Maurice, or anyone in town."

"The only support I need is from Wendy. I could take her from you, you know. I could sue you for custody—"

"Jake, please don't say something like that, even in anger."

He turned abruptly, dropping the scrap of paper onto the floor.

"Jake? Where are you going?"

"Away."

"Away where? I have to know—"

He swiveled around to face her, and she almost crashed into him. He grabbed her by the shoulders, as if he wanted to shake her, but he stopped short of actually doing it. "I can't talk about this. I'm too angry, do you understand? I'm not sure I believe you ever intended to tell me the truth, and it's beyond comprehension that you would refuse to acknowledge me as Wendy's father."

His next words nearly sliced her in two. "You're not the person I thought you were, Laurie, and right now I don't like you very much. What you did was awful, and I don't much care what your reasons were. I have to get away from here until I feel like I *can* care, until I'm not ready to strangle you."

He looked down at his hands, as if only just then becoming aware he was holding on to her. He pulled away and folded his arms, as if he were worried they might stray of their own accord toward her throat. Abruptly he spun on his heel.

"Where are you going?" she asked again, though she knew she wouldn't be able to stop him. And maybe he was right. He needed to cool off before they could discuss the problem meaningfully.

"I don't know," he said over his shoulder. He went out the front door, the closest exit, and unless she wanted to follow him outside wrapped in a towel, he was gone.

Laurie started crying in earnest. She couldn't have messed things up any better if she'd planned it this way. She unwrapped the towel from her body and stood naked in the entry hall, sniffing and blotting her tears. How could her world go from being so wonderful to so wretched in such a few short minutes?

By the time she'd dressed, pausing every half minute to wipe her eyes, Jake's truck was gone. She stood on her front porch for a long time, willing him to change his mind and come back, willing his now-familiar blue pickup to appear at the end of the driveway.

Her heart leapt into her throat when she saw a truck turning into the Folly, then fell again when she realized it was only Danny. Of all times for her brother to show up, this was one of the worst. She still hadn't forgiven him for not telling her Jake was alive, and she wasn't up to any more emotional upheaval this night.

She started to creep back into the house, turn all the lights off and pretend she wasn't home. But at the last minute she changed her mind, waving when Danny honked his horn. If anyone knew where Jake had taken off to, her brother would. Not that she intended to follow Jake. But she would feel better just knowing where he'd gone.

Danny pulled up in front of the house, cut the engine and climbed out. "I didn't expect to find you here," he said by way of greeting. "Jake said you and him were going out to dinner tonight. But I just passed him on the road, driving ninety-to-nothing like the devil was chasing him. Something wrong?"

"That's putting it mildly." She descended the stairs and stuck her hands in the pockets of her shorts as she approached her brother. "He found out about Wendy."

"Ah." Danny pulled off his hat and ran his fingers through his short, curly blond hair. "I guess he didn't take the news very well. Hell, I s'pose I never should have lied to him in the first place. If I'd told him the truth then, he wouldn't have anything to get mad about now."

Laurie almost agreed. It was so tempting to place blame on someone else. But then she shook her head. "I'm the one who should have told him, a long time ago."

Danny leaned one shoulder against his truck. "How mad is he?"

"Livid. I don't know if he'll ever forgive any of us. He was even talking about..." Her throat closed up.

"About what?"

She swallowed audibly. "About taking Wendy away from me."

"Ah, hell, Laurie, he just said that 'cause he was mad. He'd never do that. I'm sure he wouldn't do anything to hurt Wendy...or you, for that matter."

Laurie wasn't so sure about the latter. "He said I was an awful person."

"He'll get over it. And after he stews in his own juices for a while, he'll come around."

"I hope you're right."

Danny walked past her and headed for the porch. "Trust me. You got any coffee?"

She smiled and shook her head. "I'll make some." She paused as they headed indoors. "Say, Danny, would you happen to know where Jake might be headed, or how long he might stay there? He didn't take anything with him."

Danny held the screen door open for her. "Well, he's got a piece of property somewhere in the hill country. There's a house on it. He could probably stay holed up there indefinitely. That's where he went when he found out you were married."

Laurie winced inwardly at the picture of Jake in isolation, like a wounded bear taking to his cave. "How long was he gone that time?"

"Couple of weeks." She must have appeared stricken, because Danny put his arm around her shoulders, something he rarely did. "It'll be fine, Sis. You'll work it out."

While Laurie was making coffee, the phone rang. She pounced on it, hoping against hope it was Jake, but an unfamiliar man greeted her on the other end of the line. "Is Jake there?" the heavily accented voice asked.

People often called her house looking for Jake, not realizing he had a separate number, so she thought nothing of it. "He's not in," she said. "I can take a message, or I can give you his private line and you can leave a message on his answering—"

"Never mind all that," the man said gruffly. Then suddenly he asked, "Is this little Laurie?"

Laurie didn't care for his tone of voice at all. "Who's calling please?" she asked briskly.

"Tell Jake his old friend John called."

"John who?" She didn't remember any "old friends" named John.

"Just John. He'll know who I am." The line disconnected.

A chill shot through Laurie.

"What was that all about?" Danny asked.

She hung up the phone, shaken. "Someone named John. Said he was an 'old friend.'" Then a horrible thought occurred to her. "Danny, what's 'John' in Spanish?"

"It's 'Juan,' I think." Their gazes met. "Oh, Laurie, don't go borrowing trouble. Millions of people are named John. Could be someone he knew when he lived in Tyler."

Laurie nodded. But the chill sensation in her spine wouldn't leave.

Laurie just went through the motions for the next couple of days. Maurice had returned from the auction with a new mare, anxious to show her off to Jake. Laurie had had to explain the whole thing, and ever since, Maurice had been tiptoeing around her as if she were made of eggshells.

The following day her parents had returned with Wendy, who was bursting with stories about her trip to the Grand Canyon. She had a fistful of snapshots taken of her riding a little donkey, and she was eager to show them to Maurice and Jake. Once again, Laurie had to explain that Jake was gone for an indefinite period of time, and she had to endure watching Wendy's little face fall. Sure, Jake would never intentionally hurt Wendy, but did he realize he'd already hurt her with his disappearing act?

Privately, to her parents, she'd gone into more detail about why Jake had left, to which her father had replied, "And good riddance. I knew when he showed up here there'd be trouble."

"Yes, but I'm the one who caused the trouble by lying," Laurie had retorted. "I can't blame him for being angry and upset."

Her mother had nodded in agreement, completely sympathetic. Her father had said nothing.

Having Wendy back had eased some of Laurie's emptiness, but for two more days she remained restless and edgy. Jake could at least call her and let her know when to expect his return—if ever.

There had been no more phone calls from the mysterious "John," for which Laurie was eternally grateful. He probably really was an old friend.

On the fourth day of Jake's absence, Laurie and Wendy were sitting on the front porch, Wendy playing with her kittens—big lanky cats by now—and Laurie shelling peas. She heard the sound of an engine. Afraid to hope and be disappointed, she refused to look and see what, if anything, was coming up the driveway.

"Mr. Merster!" Wendy cried out. "Look, Mommy, Mr. Merster's home."

Sure enough, Jake's truck was lumbering toward them. Wendy clambered to her feet and started for the steps.

"Wait, Wendy..."

But the child didn't hear, or chose not to listen. As soon as the truck came to a stop, she tore out after it, her little legs churning, her fists pumping, eating up the distance between herself and her father.

Laurie just watched and held her breath, waiting to see how Jake would greet his daughter, now that he knew who she was.

Jake climbed out of the truck, and Laurie reveled in the sight of him. She'd missed him, of course, but until that moment she hadn't realized how much. She had the crazy impulse to do just as Wendy had—run toward him as fast as she could and throw herself at him.

Instead she walked toward him at a more sedate pace as he scooped Wendy up into his arms, seemingly unaware of Laurie's presence. Laurie stood, close but not interfering. However he chose to deal with Wendy, she wanted to know—even if she'd lost control of the situation.

"Where'd you go?" Wendy asked Jake.

"I went on a vacation—like you did," he answered easily.

"Did you go to heaven, like my daddy?" she asked with a four-year-old's innocence.

Jake's gaze flicked toward Laurie, then back to Wendy, who was perched on his hip. "No, Sunshine, I didn't go to heaven," he said with a wry smile. He'd obviously picked up "Sunshine," from Maurice. Of course he had no way of knowing that Charlie was the one who'd christened Wendy with that nickname. "Heaven's a place we'll all get to visit someday, but not this week, I hope."

Wendy seemed satisfied with his answer. "Did you go to the Grand Cannon?" she asked. "That's where me and Grandpa and Grandma Branson went."

"Nope. I went to a place called Rivercrest. It's near a big river in the hills—but not as far away as the Grand Canyon."

"Did you take pictures?" Wendy asked.

"No, but I guess I should have. It's real pretty. Maybe I'll take you there some time."

Laurie stiffened. He wouldn't take her baby anywhere, unless it was over her own dead body.

"I had my birthday. I'm four," Wendy said, holding up the requisite number of fingers.

"So I heard. Aren't birthday girls supposed to get presents?" He winked and reached into his truck through the open window. A moment later he produced a stuffed brown pony about the size of a rabbit. Wendy shrieked with delight. "It's June Bug!"

"What do you say, Wendy?" Laurie asked. Even if she was interrupting, she wouldn't allow her daughter to display bad manners.

"Oh. Thank you, Ja—Mr. Merster."

"You're welcome, Sunshine."

"Wendy," Laurie said, "why don't you take June Bug inside and get your pictures to show Mr. Mercer? I'll bet he'd like to see you riding that donkey."

Wendy nodded in agreement and wiggled to be let down. Moments later she was running full tilt toward the house, clutching her new toy with obvious delight.

Suddenly Jake and Laurie were alone with nothing but silence between them. Laurie thought of a million things she wanted to say, but the matter that troubled her most flew out of her mouth. "Are you going to tell her?"

Jake pressed his lips together in a hard line and looked up at the top of the hackberry tree that shaded the front yard. "Laurie, we have to talk."

"No kidding."

He stood straighter, folding his arms in a classic defensive posture. "I'm sure you think I did a cowardly thing by running out on you, but believe me, I needed the time away. You've had a long time to work out how you feel about all this. It was only fair you give me a few days."

She nodded her grudging agreement. "Wendy should go down for her nap in a little while. We can talk then."

Jake nodded. The screen door slammed and Wendy reappeared, her little fists full of snapshots. Laurie retreated to the shade of the front porch to finish shelling her peas. She was relatively sure Jake would reveal nothing to Wendy until he and Laurie had talked. Still, her hands trembled so violently that she ended up scattering more peas onto the porch than into her bowl.

As soon as Laurie put Wendy down for her nap, she sought out Jake. She didn't stop to comb her hair or gloss her lips, as she might have a few days ago. She didn't think about what she wanted to say. She only knew that, whatever he had in store for her, it had to be better than this waiting.

She found him in the barn, inspecting the chocolate-colored mare Maurice had bought at auction. He greeted her with a cautious nod but kept on doing what he'd been doing, which was to run his hand along every inch of the mare's skin. Laurie had seen Charlie do this. Jake was feeling for any bumps or other invisible irregularities.

"Where's Maurice?" she asked.

"Feeding the horses."

"Good, then we can talk. That is, if you don't still want to strangle me."

"I think I can resist the urge at this point." He curled the mare's lips back and examined her teeth.

"But you're still mad at me?"

"Still mad. Just not strangling mad."

Laurie gritted her teeth against the unexpected pain. What did it matter if he was mad at her? That wasn't the important issue here. "What are you planning to do about Wendy?" she asked. "Are you going to announce to the whole town that you fathered my child before we were married?"

"According to you, the whole town already knows."

"Are you going to sue me for custody? Because I'm warning you, Jake—"

"Will you just be quiet for a minute? You asked me what my plans were. Now why don't you let me answer and stop being so defensive?"

Laurie clamped her mouth shut. She folded her arms and braced herself for the worst.

"In the first place, I'm not going to rip the child out of your arms and take her away from you. You're her mother—an excellent mother, in my opinion—and separating the two of you, assuming I could even do that, wouldn't serve anyone's purpose."

With that, at least, Laurie could agree. She nodded, relaxing her jaw slightly. At least Jake wasn't going to bring to life her worst nightmare.

"But that doesn't mean I don't want a role in Wendy's life," he continued. Laurie started to object that he already had that, but he quickly added, "An official, permanent role."

Oh, dear Lord. She knew what was coming. He wanted something legal, something binding. He would insist on some court proceeding that would legally declare him to be Wendy's father. He would want to change her birth certificate, obliterating Charlie's name. He might even want to have Wendy's name changed to Mercer. And Charlie would be relegated to the role of convenient stand-in.

She couldn't let Jake do that, she just couldn't! But how could she stop him? If only he'd known Charlie the way others did. Maybe if she showed him the videos her parents had taken—

"...and I realized you were right about that."

"What?" She'd been so absorbed with her own uncomfortable thoughts, she'd lost track of what Jake was saying.

He pulled a hoof pick from his back pocket and began cleaning the complacent mare's hooves, one by one, holding each one steady between his knees as he worked on it. "Charlie was obviously a good man, and I should be eternally grateful that he stepped in when he did and took care of you and Wendy when I couldn't."

"Yes, you should," Laurie agreed quietly.

"I asked my parents about Charlie. I even asked Maurice. Everyone says he treated you like a queen, and that he couldn't have loved Wendy any more than he did. Apparently he was a family man through and through."

"And you had to hear that from other people? You didn't believe me?"

"I believed you. I didn't want to, though. I asked other people because, well, I guess I was hoping someone would contradict you, and I'd find out Charlie wasn't all that nice. Then I wouldn't have felt so guilty about...about what I want."

"Which is...?"

"Hell, Laurie, you already know. I want to claim Wendy as my daughter. To the whole world. And I don't want her calling some other man Daddy, no matter how great a guy he was."

Laurie heard the pain in his voice, and for a moment she wanted to reach out to him, to tell him he could have what he wanted, that Wendy was his. But her impulsiveness had gotten her into trouble too many times where Jake was concerned. "You can see her any time you want, you know," she said. The assurance sounded weak even to her own ears.

"That's not good enough." He'd finished with the mare's hooves, and had moved behind her to comb out her tail. "Would I be able to take her on vacation? When she starts dating, will I be able to give her boyfriends the third degree, like a proper father?

"Will she take me to the father-daughter dance?" He shook his head. "Hell, no. She might be fond of me now, but later she'll realize I'm just the hired hand. A friend of the family, maybe. And that's not good enough."

"You'll be more than that!"

"You won't even let the kid call me by my name!" Jake countered.

"We can change that. She can call you Uncle Jake. That's sort of official."

Jake was frowning, shaking his head. "I have a much better idea. While I was away, I was doing more than brooding and licking my wounds. I was thinking. And I've come up with a solution that should make everybody happy." He paused. "You and I, we'll get married."

Nine

"It's the perfect solution," Jake said, relieved now that he'd gotten his idea out into the open. He continued absently combing the horse's tail as he elaborated. "If I marry you, I'll be Wendy's stepfather—her legal guardian. No one would think twice about it if I adopted her. And I could be a real father to her, without pushing Charlie aside. Later, when she's old enough to understand, we'll explain the whole thing to her."

When all he heard from Laurie was a muffled, choking sound, he looked up to see her staring in abject horror, her hand clamped over her mouth.

"Laurie?"

She dropped her hand. "I can't believe what I'm hearing."

"What? What's wrong? You don't like the idea?" He couldn't imagine such a thing. He and Laurie were good together. From the time he'd come to the Folly, he'd had it in the back of his mind that they would finally marry and right the wrong that had been done to them so long ago. Maybe he was rushing the timetable a bit...

"Aside from the fact that it's not what I want," she said, her voice slightly shrill, "I can't believe you proposed marriage over a...a horse's rear end. You don't have a romantic bone in your body, Jake Mercer, and I wouldn't marry you now if you were the last man alive!" She spun on her heel and stalked out of the barn, her boots thudding against the packed earth.

Jake scratched his head. Well, that hadn't gone as planned, he thought, squelching the despair that threatened to engulf him. Laurie hadn't exactly leapt at the chance to marry him. Could he have been that wrong about her?

He shook his head. A few days ago he and Laurie had made love, and he'd felt closer to her than he had since he'd come back to Winnefred—maybe closer than he'd ever felt. And he'd been sure those feelings were returned. He hadn't said anything because it had been so new and fresh to him that he'd wanted to sort it out privately before opening up to Laurie.

Then he'd seen that damned calendar, and it had all come crashing down, a house of dreams built on a foundation of deceit.

A few days of lonely contemplation had put things in perspective for Jake. He was still angry with Laurie for not telling him about Wendy, and especially for her refusal to officially recognize him as the father of her child. But the more he'd thought about her explanations, the more sense they had made. She'd tried to do the right thing, just like he'd thought he was doing right by allowing her to believe he was dead.

They'd both acted out of fear, and they'd both blown it by keeping secrets they shouldn't have.

He saw no reason they couldn't start over and get past those old hurts, in time. But apparently Laurie had other ideas, if she wouldn't even consider marriage.

He finished up his inspection of the mare—Maurice had done well. Not only did the horse have beautiful confirmation and respectable lineage, but she appeared to be even tempered, a quality Folly horses were known for. Unfortunately Folly women, or one woman in particular, wasn't famous for her tranquil, tolerant nature. Jake figured he had at least a week's worth of making up ahead of him for the mistake he'd made of proposing marriage over a horse's rump.

Dinner that night was a grim affair. The tension in the air was thicker than the mashed potatoes, and the mashed potatoes could have walked out of the bowl under their own power. In fact, the entire meal did little to live up to Laurie's reputation as a good cook. The pork chops were tough, the gravy was lumpy and the fresh peas, which should have tasted like heaven, were cooked to mush. Even the rolls were overdone.

He would have liked to think that Laurie was so distracted by his manly presence that she'd been unable to pay attention to her cooking, but he suspected she'd ruined the dinner on purpose just to spite him. Jake certainly wasn't dumb enough to mention the meal's shortcomings.

"Well, Miz Laurie," Maurice said, "that was a mighty..." He stopped, unable to finish his customary praise for the evening meal. "Thanks for dinner. Filling, mighty filling."

"You're welcome, Maurice," Laurie said, though she glared at Jake, daring him to comment.

"Mommy, what happened to the peas?" Wendy asked innocently.

"What do you mean, what happened to them?"

"They're mushed, like baby food."

Laurie briefly closed her eyes. "You don't have to eat them."

Wendy, who was normally pretty good about eating vegetables, quickly laid down her fork, obviously relieved.

"Okay, look," Laurie said, addressing everyone at the table, "I know dinner was a bit under par tonight. I had an off day. But Katie brought over a pound cake this morning, and I have some ice cream. Can't mess that up. Any takers?"

"No, thanks," Maurice said, scooting his chair back. "Your sister makes a mean pound cake, but at my age I got to watch that fat intake, you know." He patted his utterly flat stomach, then stood, his thin, wiry frame seeming to mock his excuse. "Think I'll get on home." He said his good-nights, plucked his frayed straw hat from a hook by the door and escaped.

Jake was wishing he could do the same. But he would accomplish nothing by avoiding Laurie and whatever was making her so testy.

"Wendy?" Laurie asked, reaching for a covered cake dish that sat on the counter. "You like your Aunt Katie's cake, don't you?"

"No thanks, Mommy. Can I be 'scused?" she asked in an uncharacteristically timid voice.

Laurie frowned. "Sure, sweetie. I'll be in shortly to start your bath. Tell Mr. Mer—" She stopped herself. "Tell Jake good-night."

Wendy beamed, her uncertainty vanishing. "G'night, Jake." She darted over to his chair and reached up to him for a hug. He enveloped her in a quick embrace, and she whispered in his ear, "I'm glad you came back." Then she scampered off.

"See what you made me do?" Laurie said wearily. "I've driven my own child from the table."

"Our child," he said softly.

"Don't say that," she said, casting a worried eye in the direction of Wendy's disappearance.

"Not saying it isn't going to make it not true."

"I know it's true. You don't have to keep reminding me." She began clearing the dishes, avoiding his gaze.

He stood to help, but she stopped him. "I can do it. Do you want some pound cake?" she offered grudgingly as she rinsed off a plate.

Despite her protest, he took the bowls of mashed potato and pea mush to the counter and began searching the cabinets for plastic storage containers. "I don't want any cake. I want to talk."

She rounded on him. "Oh, so now you want to talk. What about when I wanted to talk, a few days ago? You weren't so willing then."

"I was angry." He quietly closed the cabinet he'd been searching. "I would have said things I'd regret."

"Well, I'm angry now. And I don't want to talk."

"Why are you angry? I'll admit, proposing marriage over a horse's rump wasn't the best idea I've ever had, but I can fix that. I can do it right."

"It doesn't matter how you do it," she said firmly. "We're not getting married."

He felt bewildered by her attitude, her inflexibility. "Why not? It would solve a helluva lot of our problems."

"It would create more than it solved. Look, Jake, four days ago you called me a liar, said you didn't like me, that I was an awful person, and you could barely keep from strangling me. Not a very good basis for a marriage.''

He'd really threatened to strangle her? When she'd said something about that earlier, he'd thought she was exaggerating. But truthfully, he barely even remembered what he'd said or done during those first few minutes after finding out about Wendy. He could recall nothing but a red haze of unreasoning, uncontrollable fury. But apparently in his temper he'd lashed out at Laurie... perhaps unfairly.

An apology now, no matter how sincere, wasn't going to sway her. He could see that by the determined set of her jaw. Even a heartfelt declaration of love, something she'd longed for when they were engaged before, wouldn't change her mind. She would see it as an attempt at manipulation, a shallow maneuver to get his way. No, he was going to have to prove to her that they belonged together, that he wanted to marry her for reasons apart from Wendy.

Unfortunately he didn't have a clue as to how to establish that proof.

''For what it's worth,'' he said, ''I'm sorry I lost my temper. I don't even remember what I said or did, but it must have been pretty bad.''

She didn't disagree with him.

''No matter what I said, you know I wouldn't hurt you.'' But obviously he had hurt her. ''Not physically, anyway,'' he amended. Could he even claim that? She still had a slight bruising below her mouth where he'd hit her in his sleep.

''There are lots of ways to hurt,'' she said, scrubbing furiously at the mashed-potato pot. ''Like when I told you how I tried to explain about Wendy earlier, and you'd fallen asleep. You didn't believe me.''

"I've thought about that," he said. "And I do vaguely remember you saying we had something important to discuss. But I was already right on the edge of sleep . . ."

She refused to look up. "I'm only sorry you couldn't believe me before, that you needed some kind of evidence."

"I know I should have listened to you," he said. "Under normal circumstances I'm always open to talking things out. These were anything but normal circumstances."

She couldn't argue with that, and she didn't.

"I realize I didn't show a lot of patience or good sense or compassion or anything that day. But no one's perfect, Laurie. I can't promise I'll never lose my cool again, but you know it's not an everyday thing with me. Don't let one incident sour our whole future."

Finally she turned to him. He was surprised to see that her eyes were filled with tears. "I accept your apology, Jake. I agree, we've both said and done some wrong things in the past few weeks. I can forgive you for running out when I needed so badly to explain myself. I can forgive the harsh words, and I can even overlook the infamous horse-rump proposal." She managed a sad little smile, but it didn't last.

"Then you'll think about it?"

She shook her head. "You forget, I've already lived through one marriage of convenience. Charlie and I cared for each other in our own way, and our mutual love for Wendy kept us together. But we were never in love ourselves. I understand that you take your responsibility to Wendy very seriously, but us getting married for her sake isn't the answer."

"Then what is the answer?" he asked, feeling bleak again.

"You don't have to marry me just to get Wendy. I was wrong to try and deny your rights in favor of Charlie's. So we'll work something out, okay? A compromise? I'm sure we can make some discreet legal arrangements—guaranteed visitation, maybe even some kind of shared custody. I want to be as fair as possible. But I don't intend for Wendy to grow up in a home with parents who aren't totally committed to each other."

Jake nodded cautiously. At least he knew where they stood. He had his work cut out for him. As for tonight, he decided to cut his losses. Laurie was in no mood to listen to his assurances that he was committed to her, to them, to the family he wanted to create.

He jammed his hat on his head. "Wendy's going to have the best of everything, Laurie," he said before sauntering out the door. And so were the two of them. Laurie just didn't know it yet.

After Wendy's bath, Laurie tucked her in with "June Bug," her new favorite toy.

"Are you mad at me, Mommy?" Wendy asked, her brow furrowed in much too serious an expression for a four-year-old.

Guilt stabbed at Laurie's heart. She absolutely couldn't let her problems with Jake hurt Wendy. "Oh, no, sweetheart." She gave her little girl a hug, inhaling the sweet scent of her freshly shampooed hair. "I know I haven't been in a very good mood lately, but it's not your fault."

"Is it Jake's fault?" Wendy asked.

Perceptive little creature, Laurie thought, amused despite herself. She thought carefully before answering, trying to couch the problems in terms her daughter could understand. "Jake and I aren't getting along real well, and that makes me a little unhappy."

"Are you gonna make him leave again?" Wendy asked, clearly worried.

Laurie shook her head. She hadn't made Jake leave the last time, but she decided not to debate the point. "Jake can stay here as long as he wants. And, Wendy, this is very important. Even if Jake and I don't always get along, that doesn't mean you can't be friends with him. In fact, I want you to always be his friend. You're very special to him."

Wendy blinked solemnly. "I know. He gave me June Bug. It's the best present I ever got." She hugged the stuffed pony.

Laurie bit back the urge to defend her gifts, a watercolor set and a computer spelling game, which she'd sent on vacation with her parents to give to Wendy when they celebrated her birthday. Both toys sat in a corner of her room, virtually untouched since her return. Maybe she wasn't quite old enough for those yet, Laurie rationalized.

The jealousy she felt toward Jake was unprecedented, and she wasn't quite ready to deal with it. Shouldn't she be thrilled that her daughter felt close to her father, even if she didn't know who Jake was?

She'd known divorced couples who constantly vied for their children's attention in a sick tug-of-war. She didn't want that to happen with her and Jake.

Then marry him, a tempting little voice whispered in her ear. Let him live in this house. Let Wendy call him "Daddy." Together she and Jake would select Wendy's birthday and Christmas gifts. Together they would make decisions about her education, summer camp, dating curfews. There would be no cause for jealousy, no reason to second-guess each other.

The fantasy was so warm and inviting—and so near, dammit—Laurie could almost wrap it around her like a blanket.

She relentlessly cut off the appealing images that bombarded her mind. Marriage was no longer an option. The moment she'd agreed to give Jake what he wanted in regard to Wendy, he'd let up on wanting her to marry him. He might have cared for her, once upon a time, but not after she'd betrayed him. Now he simply wanted to do right by Wendy.

As long as she followed through with her promise about sharing custody, Jake probably wouldn't mention marriage again, she reasoned. Such drastic measures were no longer necessary.

She looked down at her little angel, already asleep, the worry erased from her face. Wendy even smiled a little as she hugged the stuffed pony.

Laurie kissed her lightly on the forehead, vowing that she would not let her troubles with Jake affect her baby anymore. She would get along with Jake if it killed her, at least in front of Wendy.

She still loved Jake, she admitted silently. She always had, and probably always would. When he'd proposed marriage, part of her had wanted to jump into his arms and say, "Yes, yes, yes, I'll marry you," and trust that they could work out the details later.

But she knew better. She'd been married before; Jake hadn't. She knew how much work a marriage required. She knew the sacrifices as well as the benefits. As much as she wanted to, she didn't trust that Jake would be committed enough to really work at it.

Anyway, it was a moot point now. She'd given Jake what he wanted.

The flowers arrived around noon the following day—yellow roses, a dozen of them. Even as Laurie told herself not to fall victim to such a trite and shallow gesture, her woman's heart leapt with excitement.

The card read simply, "For Laurie. Love, Jake."

Love, Jake. Not only had he sent her flowers, he'd used the *L* word. He'd never before done the former, unless she counted her bridal bouquet, and he'd only said he loved her a very few times, under great duress.

After a moment's exultation, Laurie's natural suspicion kicked in. Jake had known her long enough to know which buttons to push. He wanted Wendy, and he was going to use every means within his power to strengthen the edge he'd gained last night. With this showy expression of gratitude, he was making sure she wouldn't forget her offer to give him some legal rights to Wendy.

But was it fair to accuse him of that? She'd already noticed the many changes that had taken place within Jake. From the moment he'd walked back into her life, she'd seen that he was more open, more aware of his own feelings and hers, than he'd been before. She had no doubts that he was trying to butter her up a bit, but that didn't necessarily mean he was lying about how he felt. Perhaps he really was trying to show her he cared for her.

To hell with this analysis, she decided as she put the roses in a vase and set them on a table in the living room. The flowers were gorgeous, and she was going to enjoy them. When Jake came in for lunch, she thanked him graciously and left it at that, although she did cut him an extra-large slice of pound cake.

Later that afternoon, instead of mending fences or working with the horses, he puttered around the house, progressing through a long list of repairs Laurie had prepared weeks ago. He installed new mini-blinds in the living room, put a new washer in the kitchen faucet, changed light bulbs, replaced air-conditioning filters.

It seemed as if every time she entered a room he was already there. She was practically tripping over him at every turn. She was constantly aware of his nearness, the way his soft, faded jeans hugged his long legs, and his black hair, in need of a trim, curled just so over his forehead and around his ears, inviting her touch.

Sometimes she caught his scent as he passed by her, that unique blend of soap and hay and outdoors that made her knees go weak.

She really didn't need this.

She kept wondering when he would suggest that they visit a lawyer. She wasn't crazy about this joint custody thing, but she had offered, and she would have to follow up. She would be doing the very thing she'd wanted so badly to avoid—pushing aside Charlie's role as Wendy's father. No matter how discreet they tried to be, people would eventually know that Jake had claimed his biological daughter.

Laurie would never have made this decision based on biology alone. But Jake clearly loved Wendy. He'd loved her even before he'd known she was his. And Wendy was crazy about him. She needed a daddy. Jake fit the bill.

Still, Jake never said a word about a lawyer. He just went about his work, making idle conversation if Laurie happened to be in the room, or whistling cheerfully so she could hear him if she was in another part of the house. Sometimes she could hear him talking to Wendy, who followed him around like a puppy and asked interminable questions that didn't always make sense. He was incredibly patient with her.

Jake disappeared later that afternoon, giving Laurie some breathing space as she planned and prepared dinner. But after the evening meal, he again stuck around, helping her clear the table despite her protests.

Finally she couldn't stand it anymore. She sent Wendy to the living room to watch the Disney video her grandparents had given her for her birthday. Then, as soon as Laurie was alone with Jake, she blurted out, "Jake, what are you trying to prove?"

He closed the refrigerator door and flashed her a guilty smile. "Am I that obvious?"

"You're acting very strange, like . . . like . . ."

"Like a husband?"

Oh, dear, that was exactly what came to mind. She'd never seen Jake Mercer so domestic before. And she liked it, Lord help her.

"I don't understand," she said. "I've offered to give you anything you want when it comes to Wendy. We can share custody. You can publicly announce that you're her father, if you must. She can call you 'Daddy.' So why are you still hung up on this marriage idea?"

He smiled again, and her heart flipped. "Because I said it all wrong the first time. Sure, I want to be Wendy's father. But I also want to be your husband. And I'd be damn good at the job, too."

"There's a lot more to being a husband than playing Mr. Fix-it," she said, though she was more amused than irritated by his efforts.

"I know. There's arguing about money—we do that real well already. And sharing the Sunday morning paper—no trouble there. I go for the comics and you grab the 'Today' section. I already checked that out.

"Let's see, what other potential problems do we have? I like your friends, you like mine—my best buddy is your own brother. As for in-laws—"

"Ah-ha, I've got you there," Laurie said. "My father can't stand you."

"Now, I'll admit, your daddy and me have had our differences, and I don't aim to win him over right away. But I'll treat you so good he won't have any choice but to approve of me. Pretty soon Throck and I will be going to football games together, playing golf—"

The very idea of her dignified father going to a football game, or of Jake playing golf, was so ludicrous that Laurie did something she hadn't done in days: she laughed. It felt so good she did it some more, giggling uncontrollably until tears rolled down her cheeks.

"See, if nothing else, I'll be the source of great entertainment. Married couples are supposed to laugh together, right?"

"Oh, Jake..."

"There's only one other thing that could be a source of trouble, and that's the bedroom. You know, you hear about those couples who have to go to counseling because they're sexually incompatible?" He came closer to her as he spoke, until he was standing mere inches from her.

She was no longer laughing.

"But I don't think that would be a problem for us," he said, his voice husky as he lightly stroked her cheek. "Do you?" He didn't give her a chance to answer as his mouth claimed hers.

She responded instantly, memories of their passionate afternoon together crowding her mind. Had they made love only a few days ago? So much had happened since then. Her nipples tightened as he deepened the kiss, his tongue darting in and out of her mouth. A tingling warmth bloomed deep within her, spreading to encompass her whole body.

Laurie wound her arms around his neck, pulling their bodies closer—

The phone rang.

She pulled away, masking her annoyance with a nervous laugh. "Just as well. Wendy's in the other room."

Jake released her, placing one last kiss on her forehead. "She'll have to get used to seeing her parents kiss," he said good-naturedly, as if their marriage was a foregone conclusion.

The phone was on its fifth ring by the time Laurie reached it. It was only a few steps away from where they'd been standing, but she still sounded breathless when she answered.

"Is Jake there? I know he's back from wherever he went."

Laurie instantly recognized the throaty, accented voice, and a familiar chill wiggled up her spine. "Who's calling, please?" she said stiffly, darting an apprehensive look at Jake. He was watching her intently, concern etched into his face. It amazed her that he had picked up her distress so quickly.

"You remember, little Laurie," the man said. "It's John—Jake's old, dear friend, John."

Laurie lowered the receiver and clasped her hand over the mouthpiece. "Do you know anyone named John?" she asked in a shaky voice.

Jake's eyes widened, and he took the receiver from Laurie. "Jake Mercer...hello?" He looked at Laurie, puzzled. "He hung up."

"He called once before, the night you left," Laurie said. "I meant to tell you, but I forgot. He was so... unpleasant."

"What did he say?" Jake asked, looking very worried.

"Well, the first time, he asked for you, and I explained that you weren't here and tried to give him your number at the manager's house, but he didn't want it. He just said to tell you your old friend John had called. Oh, and he seems to know who I am. He calls me 'Little Laurie.'"

"What?" Jake's face turned pale beneath his tan.

"L-Little Laurie," she said, barely above a whisper. She could tell, then, that Jake did know the mysterious caller. She suspected she knew, too. "Please don't tell me that was Juan LaBarba."

Jake nodded, looking as if he wanted to be sick.

Ten

For several seconds Laurie just stared at Jake, horrified that this awful part of his past could come back to haunt him—haunt them.

"Why is he calling you?" she finally managed to ask. "What does he want?"

"He wants me," Jake replied grimly. Then he sighed, and pulled out one of the kitchen chairs. "Sit down, Laurie. I have to tell you something."

"More secrets?" she said, almost as frightened by that as she was of Juan LaBarba himself. How many more deceptions could her battered relationship with Jake stand? She claimed the chair, glad to get off her shaky legs, and Jake sat next to her.

"Not a secret, exactly. Just something I didn't think you would want to know about, something I was planning on being done with real soon. But now you need to know. You could be in danger."

"What? Jake, you're scaring me."

He laid a comforting hand over hers. "I'm sorry, honey. I never dreamed this would lead to any kind of danger, much less that it would touch you."

"You've been working for the Marshals Service again, haven't you?" she concluded, old resentments welling up inside her. His law enforcement work had taken him away from her once. He had always viewed his duty as more important than anything, including her. Duty had almost gotten him killed. "You said you were through with all that. What happened to your wanting to be a rancher?"

"That hasn't changed. Listen to me, Laurie. I'm not working for the Marshals Service. I've been providing intelligence to the DEA, that's all."

"The Drug Enforcement Agency?" she clarified.

He nodded. "When Tom Cesore came here that day, he told me that Juan LaBarba had resurfaced, that he'd pulled his organization together and was back in business. Because I'd spent a year with him in Costa Rica, I was in a unique position to provide information. The DEA asked Cesore to talk to me."

"But you didn't have to do it," she argued.

"I wanted to help, Laurie. LaBarba is nothing better than an animal. I don't want him or his drugs near you or Wendy, or Winnefred, or anywhere. I would never feel safe knowing he's around, knowing how much he hates me. In Costa Rica I learned a lot about how he operates, how he thinks. I overheard more than he'll ever know, and what I didn't overhear I learned from Carmen. If I can help the Feds put him away, I will."

Laurie nodded, ashamed of her self-centered attitude. "Of course you should help. But that doesn't mean you have to put yourself in danger."

"Honestly, I had no intention of doing that. All I did was have a few discreet conversations with a DEA agent. I don't know how LaBarba would even know about that."

"Maybe he doesn't," Laurie reasoned. "Maybe he intended from the beginning to look you up when he came back to this area, and the information you've been providing has nothing to do with it."

"That's possible," Jake said thoughtfully, absently rubbing Laurie's hand with his thumb. "It wouldn't surprise me. He hates me, holds me personally responsible for his brother's death. The fact that I escaped his compound didn't help matters. He'd like to kill me, I think."

Jake said the words casually, but the mental image that came to Laurie's mind caused something to shift inside of her. She caught Jake's gaze and held it for uncounted seconds, taking in sharp, shallow breaths of air.

God, she loved him. The thought of losing him a second time filled her with such deep despair she could have drowned in it. And suddenly all the garbage they'd been through—the deception, the arguments, the hurtful words and her own doubts—all of it faded into insignificance.

She took his hand in both of hers, then pressed it against her cheek. "I won't let him take you away from me again," she said. "We'll change the phone number so LaBarba can't call here anymore. And then we'll let the DEA or the Marshals Service or whoever do their jobs and catch him. And you're to steer clear of the whole thing, do you understand me, Jake Mercer? You've done your part. You've given them the information they asked for. You've given enough!"

Despite the grimness of their conversation, Jake managed a crooked smile and reached for her. Before she could protest, he had pulled her onto his lap. "Laurie Branson Birkett, you're sounding suspiciously like a wife."

"I am?" she squeaked, struggling halfheartedly to escape Jake's hold.

"Uh-huh."

"Oh." She gave up the fight and relaxed, laying her head on Jake's shoulder, but her heart was pounding like a bass drum. "In that case, maybe I ought to become one."

Jake grew very still. "Was that a 'yes' I heard? You'll marry me?"

"If you'll still have me."

He hugged her so tightly she thought her ribs would crack. "Anytime, anyplace, you say."

"As soon as possible," she said. "Life's too damn short. I can't believe it's taken me so long to figure that out. Here we've been wasting all this time fighting about who's right and what's fair, hanging on to the past, to our pride, when we ought to be forgiving each other and looking toward the future."

"Amen to that."

Jake held Laurie close, allowing an alien feeling to steal over him—contentment. Laurie was warm and real in his arms, and for the first time in all the weeks since he'd been living at the Folly, they were in complete agreement, one that transcended mere physical attraction.

He reveled in the warmth of Laurie's tender feelings a few more minutes, but he knew he couldn't allow himself to get too complacent. There was still Juan LaBarba to deal with.

In her naiveté, Laurie might believe that changing her phone number and staying uninvolved would keep them safe from LaBarba, but she didn't know the man like Jake did. If he had a vendetta against Jake—and of course he did—he wouldn't give up. He would strike at Jake's most vulnerable spots until he achieved his objective, which would be nothing short of Jake's total destruction.

And the weakest link in Jake's chain was Laurie. LaBarba knew that.

Jake had unwittingly drawn Juan LaBarba into Laurie's world. Their newly built family would never be safe so long as LaBarba was free. Jake would not rest easy until his nemesis was either dead or in jail, and he intended to make that his highest priority.

Laurie knew she should have been enjoying the rehearsal dinner at her parents' country club. But all the frenzied preparations surrounding her approaching wedding with Jake was getting on her nerves. Somehow being a blushing bride just wasn't as much fun the third time around. Maybe that was because she knew what was important now—the marriage, not the wedding.

Laurie's mother had pitched a fit when Laurie had announced that she and Jake would be married in three weeks' time. "People will think you're rushing because you have to get married," Louise Branson had objected, casting a surreptitious glance at Laurie's abdomen.

Laurie had laughed. "No, Mother, I'm not pregnant. But Jake and I have waited almost five years. I don't call that rushing."

"Exactly. So what would a few more months matter?"

"You've already planned two weddings for me," Laurie had objected. "I would think you'd be tired of it by now."

"Nonsense. The first one didn't take, and the second one—well, you and Charlie practically eloped. I want this one to be right."

Laurie had remained adamant about the date she and Jake had decided on. She couldn't explain her sense of urgency. All she knew was that until she and Jake were married, she would be constantly looking over her shoulder, waiting for something to prevent the wedding and interfere with their newfound happiness.

Her mother still had managed to throw together an elaborate wedding.

Laurie just wanted it to be over. She was so looking forward to the short honeymoon Jake had planned. They were only driving to Galveston for a few days, but she couldn't wait to have him all to herself with no phones ringing or horses to be fed, no meals to be cooked or dishes to be washed—and no curious four-year-olds in constant attendance. Much as Laurie loved her daughter, she and Jake needed time alone. Time, a quiet hotel room and some uninterrupted hours of conjugal bliss. Stolen kisses behind the barn hardly made a dent in the raging fire of desire that burned inside Laurie.

She was looking forward to the wedding trip for other reasons, too. The tension of waiting for Juan LaBarba's next move was driving her crazy. Jake had put a trace on her phone line and, contrary to her stern advice, he wasn't staying uninvolved. He often disappeared for long periods of time with no explanation, and she knew he was working with the Marshals Service or the DEA.

He didn't discuss it with her because he knew it scared her.

The thought of Jake putting himself in danger made her ill with worry, but she didn't call him on it. She knew he felt it was his duty to protect her and Wendy from LaBarba, and she could hardly blame him for that. Frankly, she was frightened. The sooner LaBarba was apprehended, the better.

"That's a helluva frown for a bride to be wearing," Jake said softly into her ear. He slid his arm around her shoulders. "And you're not eating your dinner. Bridal jitters?"

She summoned a smile for him. He looked so handsome in his suit, with that one unruly shock of black hair that flopped over his forehead, defying his efforts to tame it. "I'm not the slightest bit nervous about marrying you, Jake Mercer. In fact, I've never been more sure of anything in my life."

He flashed her a grin that was pure male ego.

"Now don't let that go to your head," she warned him.

"Laurie, sweetheart, you're not going to my head so much as some other places I could mention," he whispered in her ear, then reached under the tablecloth and squeezed her thigh.

"Jake!" she said under her breath. "You've obviously had too much wine. Reverend Volker is sitting right across the table from us."

"What, you don't think Reverend Volker has ever groped his wife under a tablecloth before?"

"I'm not your wife . . . yet."

"Ah, but in a few hours . . ." He rested his chin on his hand and fixed her with a look of such adoration that she couldn't hold on to her pique.

Laurie slipped off her shoe, intending to play footsies with him. If he insisted on massaging her leg under the table, distracting her unmercifully, two could play at that game. But she never got the chance to retaliate. Jake's expression changed from a smoky look of desire to one of annoyance. He sat up straighter, then reached into his suit jacket.

"Jake, what…oh, no, you didn't bring that wretched vibrating beeper with you tonight, did you?" The beeper was how Cesore and his cohorts kept in touch with Jake when he was away from a phone.

"I had to," he said simply.

"Promise me you won't bring it to the church tomorrow!"

He smiled indulgently. "I promise. But I do need to make a phone call."

Laurie nodded glumly. "Take your time."

"I'll be right back," he said as he stood. Then he leaned down and whispered in her ear, "You're a good sport, Laurie. I love you." He strode away before she had a chance to respond.

Laurie felt herself going warm and tingly. Maybe it was the wine, but she suspected it was the fact that, for the first time in his life, Jake Mercer had voluntarily told her he loved her, without a bit of prompting. She'd been avoiding words of love, rationalizing that the words weren't important. Jake's actions showed how much he cared. Nonetheless, she'd wanted to hear him say it.

And now she had.

"Something wrong, dear?" her mother asked. Her parents were sitting to her immediate left.

"Jake had to make a phone call. Business."

Her father harrumphed. "Seems to me he could suspend business for at least a couple of days."

"He's just trying to get a few things settled before we leave on our trip. He'll be right back."

Throck shook his head. "He hasn't changed a bit, Laurie. He still puts everything in front of you."

"That's not true," Laurie said hotly. She hadn't told her family about Juan LaBarba because she hadn't wanted to panic anyone. So how could she explain that Jake's dedication to "business" was for her sake as well as his? "You forget, Daddy, that if it hadn't been for Jake I'd have declared bankruptcy by now. Whatever he's doing, it's for me and Wendy." That, at least, was true.

"He'll never make you happy," Throck said. "Mark my words."

"Oh, Throck, put a sock in it," Laurie's mother said. "She's happy for the first time in years and you're trying to spoil it." She turned to Laurie. "He can't stand to be wrong."

Laurie smiled. "Nothing could spoil this for me," she said, giving her father an affectionate pinch. "Not even a grumpy old bear. Jake has changed. He's completely devoted to me and Wendy. You'll see."

Throck's only response was to grumble something unintelligible and reach for the wine bottle. Louise intercepted it before he could refill his glass. "I think you've had quite enough," she scolded.

Jake reappeared and claimed his chair, nonchalantly refilling his own wineglass and Laurie's.

"Trouble?" she asked quietly.

"No, not exactly. Cesore says they're closing in on LaBarba. They've got him on the run now, and the trail is hot. They hope to have him in custody within twenty-four hours."

"And Cesore felt compelled to interrupt your rehearsal dinner to tell you that?" But she was smiling. The news was reassuring.

"Don't be so hard on Tom. He knows how difficult it's been to plan a wedding with this stuff hanging over our heads, and he thought that by giving us a positive progress report, we could get married without worrying about LaBarba crashing the ceremony."

Laurie shivered. That horrifying possibility hadn't crossed her mind before. LaBarba was mean enough to make that sort of grandstanding gesture. "You're right," she said, squeezing Jake's hand. "I do feel better. He'll be too busy running for his life to give us any problems."

"Exactly. Um, how soon can we shake loose from this shindig?"

"Not for a while. Why, what did you have in mind?"

His wicked smile fired her imagination. "Wendy's staying with her Aunt Katie tonight, right?"

"Now, Jake . . ."

"Don't 'Now, Jake' me. You want it as bad as I do."

"Jake!" She could feel her face heating up. But he was right. Still, she felt obligated to protest. "We've waited all this time—"

"But not out of any sense of virtue," he said, pointedly. "With your mother at the house night and day making wedding plans, and Wendy and Maurice always around . . ."

"We can last one more day," she said without much conviction.

"But why should we?"

A sense of déjà vu hit Laurie with the force of a sledgehammer.

"Laurie? What's wrong?"

"W-we've had this conversation before," she said, feeling a little bit spooked.

"You mean five years ago?" He shook his head. "Not at all the same conversation."

"The gist is the same," she said. "We were talking about jumping the gun."

"And we talked ourselves into it. I hope we do again." When she didn't respond to his teasing, he added, "You aren't superstitious, are you? History isn't going to repeat itself. Not the bad parts, anyway."

She nodded and gave him a fatalistic smile. "You're right. I'm being silly." She hooked her bare foot around his ankle. "But I'm no pushover. You'll have to work at it."

"My pleasure."

Laurie suddenly realized she was hungry. She gobbled down the rest of her dinner, fortified herself with another glass of wine and counted the minutes until she and Jake could gracefully escape.

It was close to midnight by the time they returned to the Folly. Jake was glad he'd driven; Laurie seemed a little muzzy from the free-flowing wine at the rehearsal dinner. In fact, she was downright giggly as they walked hand in hand up the steps to the front porch, dark because they'd forgotten to leave a light on.

"It's awfully late, Jake," she said as she fished in her purse for her keys. "We don't want to be dragging tomorrow, y'know? Think what a shame if we had bags under our eyes in all the wedding pictures."

"Gee, that would be a shame," Jake murmured as he draped his suit jacket over the porch railing, then proceeded to nuzzle her neck.

"As the most sober one here," she tried again, "it's your responsibility to protect my virtue."

His low, wicked laugh wasn't meant to reassure her, although he suspected she didn't really want reassurance. It wasn't as if she were a blushing virgin. They'd already been to bed together, twice if he counted that first time five years ago.

As Jake kissed her neck, inhaling the faint residue of her honeysuckle perfume, she made one more attempt. "We really should wait...oh!"

"What?"

"Déjà vu again," she murmured. "Don't you remember?"

"I seem to remember that you were the most tempting woman I'd ever seen, and I was fighting for my self-control," he replied. "We were standing on the front porch of your little apartment with a yellow bug light glaring down on us."

"True," she said. "But your so-called efforts at self-control were token at best."

"Same as yours tonight. If you really want to wait until tomorrow night, just say, 'Jake, go home.' And I will."

"Jake..." She paused dramatically. "What am I doing? I don't want to wait. A girl could spend her whole life waiting." Her voice was husky as she added, "Who cares about déjà vu, anyway?"

"That's what I thought." He claimed her mouth, tunneling his fingers through her hair, which she'd allowed to grow to shoulder length. She maintained it was because Wendy was past the hair-pulling stage, but he suspected she'd done it for him. He missed the waist-length hair she'd worn as a girl.

"Why don't you make another stab at finding those keys?" Jake murmured against her lips.

In answer she dropped her purse onto the porch with a thud. "I like it out here. There's a cool breeze, the crickets are chirping—"

"The mosquitoes are biting."

"I haven't felt a single mosquito," she argued good-naturedly as she loosened his tie. "Have you?"

"Let me get this straight," he said as he reached behind her and began unfastening the long row of buttons down her back. "You want to make love on the front porch."

"On the porch swing," she clarified.

"You want to get splinters in your—"

"It has a cushion." She kicked off her high heels and took him by the hand. "This way. Any objections?"

"Where's Maurice?" he asked warily.

"In bed and asleep hours ago. You know he never stays up past ten. Anyway, we passed his house on the way in. Dark and quiet."

"In that case, no objections." And no déjà vu, either. His virginal Laurie hadn't been nearly this adventurous. He was going to love being married to her.

By the time they reached the swing, he'd discarded his shoes, belt, tie, and had his cuffs undone. He swiveled Laurie around so he could finish her dress buttons, then slid the garment off her shoulders and down. She was wearing one of those slinky underthings designed to drive men wild, and it did the trick, all right. Jake molded his hands around her waist, then slid his arms forward and across her ribs to cup her breasts.

She moaned and leaned against him, her soft hair tickling his neck. Her bottom rubbed against his arousal, and he had to bite his lip to keep from tearing that wispy thing off of her and taking her right then and there.

He'd never been one for pretty words, a shortcoming that had once bothered Laurie enough that she'd complained. Back then he'd argued that actions speak louder than words. But as he held her against him now, caressing her breasts, burying his face in her hair, he suddenly realized that actions weren't enough. He wanted her to know how he felt. And he wanted to hear pretty words from her, too.

"Earlier tonight I told you I loved you," he said.

"Yes."

"Is that all the reaction I get?"

"I've been savoring the experience," she said in a dreamy voice.

"You don't have to savor it. I'll say it every day, at least. And I'll mean it, too."

She turned to face him, twining her arms around his neck. "I've waited a long time to hear you say that. But you don't have to do it to please me, you know. I understand now what you meant all those years ago. What you do is much more important than what you say. You've shown me you love me."

"But I want to say it, too. I love you, Laurie, and I'll never leave you again, not for any reason."

"I love you, too, Jake. I suppose I always have, even when I hated you. You have a hold over me."

He kissed her lightly, then more seriously, plunging his tongue into her mouth, kneading her bottom with both hands, pulling her hard against him. He broke the kiss just long enough to say, "If you really love me, you'll get out of those panty hose."

He finished undressing as he watched her shimmy out of her slip and her pale stockings. In the darkness he couldn't make out every detail of her nakedness, just enough to send his imagination into overdrive. She pulled the camisole over her head, revealing the pale gleam of her breasts. Her whole body was in breathtaking silhouette, light and dark shadows against the blackness of the night, and he ached for her.

Instead of coming to him, she sat on the porch swing, then reclined, swinging her long legs onto the seat.

"And where am I supposed to sit?" he asked, stepping out of his briefs until he was as bare as she.

"On top of me, of course," she said with a saucy toss of her head.

"You'll have to make room." He lifted her foot and brought it to his lips, kissing the instep, the ankle, the calf. Slowly he worked his way up her leg, gratified by the sound of her breathing coming in quick little gasps.

When he reached the apex of her thighs he began to tease her with his tongue, managing to arouse himself at least as much as Laurie. They reached the limit of patience at about the same time, and she practically dragged him to lie on top of her, propping one of her legs on the back of the swing to make room for him.

She was warm and slick when he entered her. He tried to go slowly, but his thin thread of self-restraint suddenly snapped, and he drove deeply into her with a hard, fast rhythm. She matched him thrust for thrust, crying out his name as he clutched her shoulders and released everything into her—his love, his seed, his soul.

They both went still, though the porch swing continued to move back and forth in a lazy cadence that belied the frenzied coupling that had just taken place.

"A little too anxious, maybe?" he asked when he could talk.

She laughed. "Who, me or you?"

"Me. I got carried away."

"So did I. Carried away to a wonderful, perfect place."

"I'm too heavy for you," he said, attempting to shift his weight off of her.

"No," she said, holding him tight. "Just let me enjoy having you squash me a few more minutes."

"I'm sweating on you."

"Horses sweat. Men perspire. Women glow."

"Yeah, well, I notice you're glowing quite a bit."

She pinched his ear. "Very unchivalrous of you to point that out. But you're right, air-conditioning sounds pretty good right about now."

Reluctantly they moved from the swing—not the most comfortable venue for lovemaking, they'd discovered—and picked up their clothes. Laurie found her keys and let them inside.

"You can stay the night if you promise we can sleep," she said. "I'd like to be alert while I'm pledging my whole life to you."

"Wouldn't look good if we fell asleep in the wedding cake," he agreed.

Still, after they'd slid between cool sheets, Jake reached for her. She thought she would fall asleep in his arms, but he began idly stroking her here and there, awakening her body, enlivening her imagination, until sleep was impossible. They made love again, slowly, leisurely, and Jake convinced Laurie that losing a few winks wasn't such a bad thing.

Eleven

Something pulled Laurie out of a deep sleep. She looked first at Jake, who was dozing peacefully beside her, and smiled as she recalled the previous night. She smiled even wider as she remembered that today was her wedding day.

The doorbell pealed, and she realized that must have been what woke her. Her bedside clock said it was after nine. She needed to be up, anyway. She grabbed a robe from the back of the closet door and wrapped it around her, then hurried to the door.

The bell rang a third time before Laurie reached it. "All right, I'm coming," she called out. When she pulled the door open, she found her parents standing on the front porch. Her mother was holding a long garment bag.

Egad, she only hoped she could get rid of them before Jake came wandering out of the bedroom. It was bad enough his truck was parked out front instead of closer to his own house.

"Good morning, good morning," Louise greeted her daughter cheerily. "I finished the hem on your dress and wanted to get it over here nice and early, so you aren't rushed on your special day."

Laurie refrained from reminding her mother that, since this was her third such "special day," it was losing its novelty. Instead she summoned a sleepy smile. "Come in. What's in Daddy's bag?" she asked, eyeing the white paper sack her father held.

"Bagels and strawberry cream cheese—your favorite," Louise said as she whisked herself inside. "It's a peace offering, of sorts. Your father has something to say to you."

"Oh?" was all Laurie said as they all walked into the kitchen. She headed straight for the coffee maker. How could she be expected to handle her parents this early in the morning without caffeine?

"I'm sorry I criticized your choice of husband last night," her father said, quickly and gruffly, and probably under protest, Laurie figured. "You're a smart girl, and if you really believe that he's changed, that he'll put you and Wendy first, then who am I to argue? Although—"

"Throck, don't ruin it," Louise said as she put the bagels on a plate.

Laurie flipped on the coffee maker, then went to her father and kissed him on the cheek. "Thank you, Daddy. I do want you and Jake to get along. It'll all work out, you'll see. Wendy adores him."

"And what about Charlie?" her father asked. "I thought she adored him."

Laurie had done a lot of thinking about that. "Wendy doesn't even remember Charlie. All she knows of him is his picture, and what we've told her about him, and that's pretty abstract. Jake's here, Daddy. Charlie isn't. But Charlie wouldn't have wanted his little girl to grow up without a dad. And I know he would approve. I hope none of us ever forgets the role Charlie played in our lives, but it's time to move on."

"Of course it is," Louise added soothingly.

Seeing the doubtful look on her father's face, Laurie might have elaborated, but the phone rang. "Now what?" she grumbled as she reached for the phone. "Hello?"

"Good morning, Laurie. Hope I didn't wake you."

"Tom." By now she knew Tom Cesore's voice before he identified himself. Lord knew he'd called the house often enough when he couldn't locate Jake any other way.

"Is Jake there? I really need to speak to him."

Laurie could feel the heat rising in her face. "Tom, it's our wedding day. Whatever it is can wait."

"I'm sorry, Laurie, but it can't. Jake made me promise to leave him alone today of all days, but this is an emergency. Is he there?"

Panic welled up in Laurie's throat. This couldn't be happening! If Tom wanted Jake to go somewhere, do something... But no, Jake wouldn't. He wouldn't dare. He would tell Tom no, whatever it was. Secure in that knowledge, she replied, "I'll go get him."

She propped the receiver on top of the phone and, with an apologetic nod toward her parents, because she was probably about to offend their sensibilities, she headed for the bedroom.

Jake was still asleep, sprawled diagonally across her king-size bed. She shook his shoulder none too gently. "Jake, wake up."

"Huh?"

"Tom Cesore is on the phone and insists on talking to you. But before you grab that phone," she said, arresting his attempt to pick up the receiver from the phone on the nightstand, "I might remind you that we're getting married in less than four hours. And if you intend to let Tom pull you into something on this of all days, then don't bother to show up at the church, 'cause I won't be there!"

"Let's see what he wants first," Jake said sensibly, rubbing his face. He reached for the phone again, and this time she didn't stop him. "Tom? What's going on?"

Laurie stepped out into the hall and called to her mother to hang up the kitchen phone. When she returned to the bedroom, Jake was sitting on the edge of the bed, still half-wrapped in the blanket. He was listening, nodding and frowning.

Laurie watched, chewing her fingernail. She could tell by the look on Jake's face that something was terribly wrong, that he was upset, and she immediately regretted her harsh words.

"I'll have to call you back," he finally said in a rough voice before hanging up.

"Oh, Jake, what is it?" she asked, sitting beside him and taking his hand.

"Talk about déjà vu," he murmured, looking as if he couldn't quite believe what was happening. "They've caught up with Juan LaBarba. He and some of his gang are holed up in a house outside of Tyler, in a standoff with the DEA."

"That's good, isn't it?" Laurie asked. "I mean, they've got him! Surely they...oh, Jake, they don't need you, do they?"

Jake looked at her then, and the tortured expression on his face was enough to bring tears to her eyes. "He's holding his own wife hostage, Laurie."

"Carmen? He's holding Carmen?" In the bits and pieces she'd gleaned from Jake about his time in Costa Rica, Carmen had played a prominent role. Juan's wife had nursed Jake back to health, shielded him from the worst of her husband's wrath, provided him with privileged information and in the end had helped him escape. Jake owed her his life.

Jake nodded. "They're bringing in a hostage-negotiation team. But LaBarba says he won't talk to anyone but me."

"I see" was all Laurie could manage.

Jake grasped her by the shoulders. "Do you?"

"Yes, Jake, I really do. You have to go."

"I don't have to," he said softly. "It's my choice. And frankly, if my leaving means losing you, then I'll stay."

"Oh, Jake." She caressed his cheek as tears spilled down her face. "It's a lovely sentiment, but if you allowed anything to happen to Carmen just so you could please your self-centered bride, you wouldn't be the man I fell in love with." It occurred to Laurie then that she'd just put an end to the déjà vu. Five years ago, when Jake made a similar announcement, she had responded with petulance, resenting his duty. Now, she saw his duty as so much a part of him that she had to love it along with the rest of him.

"Then you'll wait for me at the church?" he asked.

"With bells on. You do what you have to do to help Carmen. The wedding will keep."

"I really do love you, Laurie." He gave her a quick kiss, then reached for the phone to call Tom back. Halfway through dialing, he paused. "On second thought, put some clothes on."

"Why?"

"Just do it. History might be repeating itself, but that doesn't mean I have to make the same mistake twice."

"What are you talking about?" she asked, but just the same she began rummaging in her closet for something she could throw on. She settled on a red sundress.

He completed his phone call before answering her question, walking up behind her as she faced the closet and putting his arms around her. He was still naked. "Before I face LaBarba, we're going to be legally hitched." He placed a gentle hand on her abdomen. "We didn't use any protection last night. You could be pregnant again."

"And you don't want to leave me an unwed mother a second time? Is that supposed to be comforting? That you'd rather I be your widow?"

"I'm not going to get killed. I just..." He swiveled her around in his arms until she faced him. "I just want us to be married before I leave for Tyler. We can say the vows again later at the church, in front of the whole town. What harm will it do to say them twice?"

When Laurie would have argued further, he added, "Do it for me, please?"

She nodded, then added, "I lost you once, Jake Mercer. If anything happens to you, I'll—"

"Nothing's going to happen. Now put that dress on."

"A red wedding dress," she groused, though she did as he asked while he put on his own clothes. "I never imagined I would get married without taking a shower first."

Laurie's mother showed little reaction when Laurie and Jake emerged from the bedroom, but her father puffed up like a rooster ready to fight.

Laurie forestalled the diatribe he was about to launch. "There's an emergency, and Jake has to leave," she said. "He might not get to the church on time for the wedding—"

"He's not going anywhere!" Throck finally exploded, advancing on Jake with a murderous glint in his eye. "If you think you're going to sleep with my daughter, then leave her standing at the altar—"

"I'm not," Jake said, facing his irate future father-in-law with what Laurie thought was unbelievable composure. "We're going to Reverend Volker's house right now to tie the knot. I don't have time to explain, but there's a slight chance I won't make it to the wedding. If that happens, I want Laurie and me to be married."

"You're getting married now?" Louise wailed.

"Don't worry, Mother, we'll do it again later at the church," Laurie said as she grabbed her purse. "This is just Jake's idea of an added precaution, probably totally unnecessary." She gave Jake a meaningful look.

"If you'd like to be witnesses, follow us to the reverend's house," Jake said as he turned, his hand at Laurie's waist, and guided her toward the front door. Her parents had no choice but to follow, still sputtering halfhearted objections. The fact that Jake was determined to go through with the vows no matter what had apparently mollified her father somewhat.

On the front porch, Louise caught up with Laurie and pulled her aside. "Sweetheart," she whispered, gesturing discreetly toward something under the porch swing, "you might want to tidy up out here some time soon."

Laurie was mortified as she realized her mother was pointing at a pair of panties.

The ceremony was short and sweet. Reverend Volker, unshaven and flustered, nonetheless performed the wedding in his living room with quiet dignity as his confused wife looked on. Jake spoke his vows in a clear, sure voice, knowing that with Laurie as his wife he would be better equipped to handle whatever the rest of the day brought. He fervently hoped that the business with LaBarba would be concluded quickly and he would make it back in plenty of time for the church wedding. But if he didn't, at least no one would think it was because he didn't want to marry Laurie.

Laurie's voice shook as she pledged her life to his, but she gripped his hand tightly and smiled. They'd forgotten the rings, so they skipped that part of the ceremony. Reverend Volker pronounced them husband and wife, and they kissed briefly, self-consciously.

Then Jake had to leave. There was no time for elaborate goodbyes, which were probably unnecessary, anyway, he rationalized. He would be seeing her again in a few hours. Still, getting into his truck and driving away, leaving his wife of five minutes behind, was the hardest thing he'd ever done.

Laurie's sense of déjà vu was back with a vengeance as she relived the beginnings of her worst nightmare. Here she was in the bride's room at her family's church with her parents and her sister, Katie. It was hot, and her demure ecru lace dress was about to choke her. The smell of roses was nauseating. And once again, Jake was thirty minutes late.

No one knew quite what to say, but they tried, anyway. "I'm sure it couldn't possibly be the same as last time," Katie said in a choked voice, her hand on Laurie's shoulder. "I mean, that would be just too weird."

"At least we know it's not cold feet," Throck said, a sentiment which was not at all helpful.

"Who has cold feet?" Wendy asked. She looked so precious in her flower-girl dress and her shiny patent leather shoes.

Heedless of wrinkling her own dress, Laurie pulled her daughter into her lap. The little girl's presence was a welcome reminder that not *everything* was the same as it had been five years ago.

"Cold feet is nothing we have to worry about," she said.

"But where's Jake?"

"He's coming," Laurie said, showing her usual optimism, though she knew, beyond the shadow of a doubt, that Jake would be here if he could—or he would have called to let her know what was happening. The fact that no one had called was ominous.

The door to the bride's room opened and her brother stepped inside, followed by Jake's parents wearing grim expressions. Laurie set Wendy down and was instantly on her feet. "Danny?"

He shook his head. "I can't find out anything beyond the fact that there's a standoff."

"No news is good news, right?" Louise said. Throck gave her a sour look.

Laurie consulted her watch and came to a decision. "We can't wait any longer. I'll explain to the guests that Jake and I are already married, that he was called away on an emergency, and I'll invite everyone to the reception. Then, when he shows up, we can celebrate and cut the cake and take pictures, and it will all work out.''

By the expressions on everyone's faces, they didn't believe her any more than she believed herself. Still, what choice did they have? She headed out the door and into the church, and her worried family followed. Wendy, bewildered by the turn of events, began to cry because she wasn't allowed to walk down the aisle with her flower basket ahead of her mother, as they'd rehearsed last night.

Laurie appeased her daughter by taking her hand and letting her walk with her to the front of the church. As she moved quietly, steadfastly forward, without benefit of music, and with no groom waiting at the altar, a spate of whispering broke out among the wedding guests. Laurie could just imagine what they were thinking, which probably wasn't any wilder than the true situation.

She didn't really care what they thought. She just wanted to get this ordeal over with and go home to wait for Jake. The whole thing seemed surreal to her, like a recurring nightmare. But surely the outcome wouldn't be the same. Not this time. God couldn't be that cruel.

Close to tears, Laurie stood before the assembled guests and took a deep breath. "There's been a slight change of plans," she began, her voice quavering. "Due to unforeseen circum—" She stopped when Wendy pulled on her skirt and pointed toward the back of the church, where there was a flurry of activity.

"Mommy, look!"

Laurie's heart was in her throat as a man in a tuxedo emerged from the crowd of people at the back door. It was Jake!

"Thank you, God," she said out loud, which caused a titter of nervous laughter. Then she addressed the congregation again, this time grinning ear to ear. "On second thought, there will be no change of plans at all." And then she couldn't contain herself any longer. She ran up the aisle, where Jake met her halfway, and launched herself into his arms.

"Easy, honey," he said in an oddly strained voice.

"Oh, Jake, I'm so glad you're here," she said, showering his face with kisses that left lipstick smears. "I was so afraid something awful had happened. Why didn't you call?"

"Uh, maybe we should get this show on the road," he said, nodding toward their expectant guests.

"Oh, yeah. I guess I can grill you later."

The organist started the music, and the procession was quickly reassembled. The parents hurriedly sat in their assigned pews. Wendy, her little face beaming, walked down the aisle a second time throwing rose petals with abandon. And finally the bride, trembling with joy, made her rather unsteady way up to the altar to join the groom.

Wendy grabbed on to Jake's leg and refused to let go. Rather than incite a tantrum, Laurie allowed her to hold on to Jake as they recited their vows. She didn't care, so long as she got to hold on to him, too.

Jake's face was tight and pale as he repeated what the reverend told him to say, his voice much less sure than it had been this morning. Laurie wondered briefly why that was, but then she had her own vows to repeat and a ring to fumble with, and she didn't worry about it.

It seemed like an eternity, but finally Reverend Volker issued those five wonderful words, "You may kiss the bride." Laurie didn't hesitate. She was no blushing bride. She grasped Jake by the shoulders and kissed him for all she was worth, eager to show the world how much she loved this man.

She was just beginning to wonder why his response was so tepid when his knees buckled and he collapsed to the floor, unconscious. His tuxedo jacket fell open, revealing a crimson stain spreading obscenely across his snow white shirt.

"Don't you dare die, Jake Mercer. I'll kill you if you die!"

Jake heard Laurie's words, but he couldn't quite summon the motor skills necessary to open his eyes and respond. He remembered that he'd been shot. He recalled arguing with the paramedics that he couldn't go to the hospital yet, that he had an important promise to keep first. So they'd patched him up as best they could, issuing dire warnings all the while. Cesore had driven him back to Winnefred, cursing Jake's stubbornness. They'd stopped by Jake's house so he could change into his tuxedo—not without some degree of pain. He'd shaved in the car on the way to the church.

But, by God, he'd made it to the wedding and he'd kept his promise to Laurie. They'd repeated their vows before the whole town, and they were husband and wife in everyone's eyes. At least, he was pretty sure they'd gone through with the ceremony. His memory started to get a little fuzzy right about then.

Laurie, his beloved wife. Why was she yelling at him?

"You're a complete idiot, do you know that? Why didn't you go straight to the hospital? You know I would have understood. I can forgive you anything, anything, except dying.

"I said that once before, the first time you got shot," she continued, her anger receding for a moment. "I guess history really does repeat itself."

"Huh-uh," he murmured, cracking first one eye, then the other, open to the harsh hospital lights.

Laurie froze, staring at him with big eyes. "Jake? Are you there?"

"Mm-hm. Hist'ry doesn't repeat . . ." That was all he could manage for the moment.

"Don't try to talk, okay?" she said, suddenly all concern as she took his hand. "Just squeeze if you understand."

He squeezed. But he was becoming more alert by the second. And aside from a burning pain in his side, he didn't feel all that bad. Certainly not as bad as the last time he'd been shot, when Juan LaBarba had thrown him into the back of a bouncing truck to bleed to death. "I'm fine," he said. "I can talk."

"Sure you're fine. Next time you take a bullet in the gut, try to remember that I'd much prefer a broken promise to a dead husband, okay?"

"Okay," he said meekly. His mouth felt as if it was full of cotton. "Can I have some water?"

She poured him a glass from the pitcher on the bedside table. He was amazed to discover he couldn't sit up. He sipped the water through a straw.

"Better," he said. "You know what happened?"

"Tom gave me the *Reader's Digest* condensed version. He said LaBarba offered to release Carmen in exchange for you. And you agreed."

"Yeah. You mad?"

"No, of course not. I'll only be mad if you die."

"I'm not going to die." He was fairly sure of that now. He felt as if he had a pretty firm grip on life. "I didn't just offer myself up as a sacrifice, you know,'' he said. "We had a plan. And I was wearing a bullet-proof vest."

"Oh, that did a lot of good."

"We weren't counting on the sniper LaBarba had hidden up on the roof—or the Teflon bullets."

"Cop killers," Laurie said, referring to the bullets. "They can slip right through those vests."

Didn't Jake know it. "It was just a flesh wound," he said. "It didn't bleed that much."

"The bullet nicked your spleen. You almost bled to death internally. You just got out of surgery a little while ago."

"Oh." After thinking a moment, he asked, "Did you know they killed LaBarba?"

She nodded. "Tom said the moment that first bullet flew, LaBarba didn't stand a chance. They weren't about to let him get away again. I just feel sorry for Carmen, having to watch."

"She won't mourn him for long, trust me. She hated him. Now she's free." He thought for a moment, then asked, "Did they take out my spleen? I was kind of attached to it."

"No, it's still there. Most of it."

"Oh," he said again. "Laurie, I'm really sorry."

"For what?"

"For ruining our wedding day. Again."

She smiled. "It's not ruined as far as I'm concerned." She wiggled her fingers in front of his face, showing off her gold band. "We got hitched, didn't we? That's the important part. The rest is just window dressing."

"You're really not mad?"

"Of course not. Although I'm not real thrilled about spending our honeymoon in a hospital."

"When I get out of here, we'll have a real honeymoon, I promise."

"And we all know Jake Mercer keeps his promises, right?" She leaned over and kissed him gently.

Even in his debilitated condition, his body responded. He'd be ready for that honeymoon sooner than anyone expected. "I love you, Laurie," he said in a husky voice.

"I love you, too, Jake," she said, her eyes brimming with tears. "You're my hero. Nothing and no one is going to take you away from me again."

"Amen to that," he said before drifting off again, a smile on his lips.

Epilogue

The annual town picnic, held in Winnefred's city cemetery, seemed as good a time as any to take Wendy to visit Charlie's grave. As with many small Texas towns, each year the citizens gathered at the graveyard to trim hedges, pull weeds and plant flowers, as well as feast on barbecue and other Southern delicacies.

Laurie had never taken Wendy to visit Charlie's final resting place because she thought it might upset her, or that she plain wouldn't understand. But now that she was almost six—and quite precocious—Laurie figured it was okay. Besides, with all the laughter and eating and games going on, with children playing tag among the headstones, today the cemetery was a happy place.

Wendy stood before the granite headstone, solemnly reading the words engraved there—with help from her mother.

"What does 'beloved' mean?" Wendy asked.

"It means we loved him very much."

"Was it sad when he died?"

"Yes, very sad."

"Like when Princess died?"

Princess was the old mother barn cat who'd given birth to the kittens Wendy had adopted and tamed.

"Well, something like that," Laurie replied. "But sad times are part of life. We just have to help each other get through them, and then go on."

"It wasn't sad for Daddy Charlie, 'cause he got to go to heaven," Wendy said. "And someday I'll see him there."

"If you're a good girl," Laurie teased, tweaking her daughter on the nose.

Wendy laughed, but then she grew solemn again. She ran her hand over the engraved lettering. "He's my real daddy, right?"

"Yes."

"And Daddy is my stepfather."

"No, Jake is your real daddy, too. You're a lucky little girl to have two real daddies."

Wendy put her hands on her hips. "Huh-uh. Harry Thomason says you can only have one real daddy, that a man has to plant a seed and grow a baby tree. Did Daddy Charlie plant my seed, or did Daddy?"

Good heavens! Laurie was sure she had never asked such questions of her mother, not when she was six or sixteen. She pondered the matter a moment before answering.

"There's a lot more to being a father than planting a seed. It's kind of like our flower garden. Planting the seeds is just the first step. You have to water, and spray for bugs, and pull weeds, or you won't have much in the way of flowers. Jake planted your seed. But when he couldn't be here, Daddy Charlie helped me take care of you. He fed you and changed your diaper and bathed you—"

"Did he spray me for bugs?"

Laurie smiled. "No, you didn't have any bugs. And there's no such thing as a baby tree. Babies grow inside mamas' tummies."

"Like with the horses?" Wendy asked. A child didn't grow up on a stud farm without absorbing some facts of life. She'd already witnessed a foal being born, with Laurie fluttering and fussing the whole time, afraid that the sight would disturb her daughter. But Wendy had taken it all in stride.

"Exactly like with the horses," Laurie confirmed. "Seems to me we've talked about this before. Remember your teacher Mrs. Tennyson who had the baby last year? Remember how her tummy got big?"

"Oh, yeah, I think I remember."

"Anyway, you'll get to see it happen firsthand, pretty soon," Laurie murmured, more to herself than Wendy.

They planted the petunias Laurie had brought for Charlie's grave, working in contented silence. Someday Laurie would have to go into more detail about Wendy's parentage, before she found out the truth from some loudmouthed kid. But for now, she felt satisfied that she had answered Wendy's questions truthfully, in a way she could understand.

"I'm hungry," Laurie announced as Wendy patted the dirt around the last petunia.

"So am I," said a deep voice behind them. Laurie turned to see Jake leaning against a red oak tree, arms folded, eyes appraising, and she knew he was thinking about more than barbecue. So was she. They'd had a lovely, lusty morning encounter interrupted earlier by an impatient little girl wanting to get to the picnic early.

"Daddy, come see Daddy Charlie's grave," Wendy announced proudly. "He has the biggest stone here, and me and Mommy planted flowers."

"Yes, I see that," Jake replied. "They look very nice. I'm sure Charlie is real proud of them."

Over the past two years Jake had completely gotten over any jealousy or competitiveness he'd once felt for Charlie Birkett, partly because Laurie made sure every day of her life that Jake knew how much he was loved.

Jake turned to Laurie. "Are y'all done here? 'Cause if you're not, I can—"

"No, we're done. I was just about to suggest we go find the food before it's all gone."

"That's why I came looking for you," Jake said. "The hot dogs are disappearing fast. Wendy, maybe you better run on ahead and save us a couple."

"Okay, Daddy. Bye, Daddy Charlie," she said with a careless wave to the headstone before running off.

Jake put his arm around Laurie's shoulders as they followed at a more leisurely pace. "Sounds like that went okay."

"You didn't hear the part where she asked which of her daddies planted the baby tree. The next time she asks something like that, you get to help me explain."

"Gladly. Um, before we join the others . . ." He drew Laurie into the shade of a huge mimosa tree. "Isn't there something you'd like to tell me?"

"Uh . . . actually there is." She hadn't wanted to mention it to Jake until she was a hundred percent sure. During the past two years they'd been trying to have another baby, and she didn't want to raise anyone's hopes if it turned out to be a false alarm. But she'd gotten up early every morning for the past five days to perform an at-home pregnancy test, and every one had come up positive.

She supposed it was safe to tell Jake. Then she realized she wouldn't have to. He was grinning ear to ear.

"You already know," she said, putting her hands on her hips. "How? I haven't told a soul, and I hid those pregnancy tests real good. I even drove into Tyler to buy them."

He laughed at that. "You forget, I know every delicious inch of your body and I notice the slightest change. I also noticed you're about two weeks late."

"Well, really! Men aren't supposed to keep track of things like that."

"I keep track of anything that affects our sex life." Abruptly the teasing banter stopped. "Are we really gonna have another baby?"

Laurie nodded, barely containing her elation. "Five different brands of pregnancy test can't be wrong. I have a doctor's appointment on Monday, but I already know."

"Laurie." His voice was husky with emotions he no longer denied or tried to hide from her. "I love you. And I can't wait to meet our new kid. Wendy's the greatest, and I'd have been perfectly satisfied with just her, you know."

"I know."

"But I am looking forward to seeing you get fat."

"You won't be disappointed, then. Last time I blew up like the Hindenburg."

"I want to be there for you during labor."

"It's not a pretty sight. I'm not a good sport about pain."

"I want to hold the baby and feed him and change his diaper and do all those daddy things I missed the first time."

"Good. The 2:00 a.m. feedings are all yours."

He took her teasing in stride. "I'll be the most incredibly good father."

"You're already an incredibly good father, not to mention husband, lover, provider."

"Especially lover," he said, giving her a gentle kiss that nonetheless promised better things to come later, when they were alone.

Laurie reveled in the kiss, brief but potent. She felt so incredibly lucky, with blessings she counted every day— a lovely daughter and another child on the way, a prospering ranch, friends, family. But at that moment, she was most thankful for the second chance she'd been given with Jake. This time around, however, she knew nothing could come between them, not honor or duty or pride. The prodigal groom had come home, and she would hold him close forever.

*   *   *   *   *

COMING NEXT MONTH

#1009 THE COWBOY AND THE KID—Anne McAllister

July's *Man of the Month*, rodeo cowboy Taggart Jones, vowed never to remarry, but his little girl had other plans for him—and every one involved feisty schoolmarm Felicity Albright.

#1010 A GIFT FOR BABY—Raye Morgan

The Baby Shower

All Hailey Kingston wanted was to go to her friend's baby shower. Instead, she was stuck on a remote ranch, with a handsome cowboy as her keeper. But the longer she stayed in Mitch Harper's arms, the less she wanted to leave!

#1011 THE BABY NOTION—Dixie Browning

Daddy Knows Last

Priscilla Barrington wanted a baby, so she planned a visit to the town sperm bank. But then she met Jake Spencer! Could she convince the rugged cowboy to father her child—the old-fashioned way?

#1012 THE BRIDE WORE BLUE—Cindy Gerard

Northern Lights Brides

When Maggie Adams returned home, she never expected to see her childhood neighbor Blue Hazzard. Could the former gawky teenager turned hunk teach Maggie how to love again?

#1013 GAVIN'S CHILD—Caroline Cross

Bachelors and Babies

Gavin Cantrell was stunned to return home and learn that his estranged wife Annie had given birth to his child without telling him. Now that he was back, would his dream of being a family man be fulfilled?

#1014 MONTANA FEVER—Jackie Merritt

Made in Montana

Independent Lola Fanon never met anyone as infuriating—or as irresistible—as Duke Sheridan. She knew he wasn't her type, but staying away from the handsome rancher was becoming a losing battle....

BEGINNING IN APRIL
FROM

SILHOUETTE® Desire®

The Wedding Night

Three passion-filled stories about what happens when the wedding ring goes on...and the lights go out!

In April—A kidnapped bride is returned to her husband in
FORGOTTEN VOWS by Modean Moon

In May—A marriage of convenience turns into so much more in
INSTANT HUSBAND by Judith McWilliams

In June—A once-reluctant groom discovers he's a father in
THE PRODIGAL GROOM by Karen Leabo

THE WEDDING NIGHT: The excitement began when they said, "I do."

SILHOUETTE® *Desire*

MAN of the MONTH 1996

He's tough enough to capture your heart,
Tender enough to cradle a newborn baby
And sexy enough to satisfy your wildest fantasies....

He's Silhouette Desire's MAN OF THE MONTH!

From the moment he meets the woman of his
dreams to the time the handsome hunk says *I do...*

Fall in love with these incredible men:

In July:	*THE COWBOY AND THE KID* by Anne McAllister
In August:	*DON'T FENCE ME IN* by Kathleen Korbel
In September:	*TALLCHIEF'S BRIDE* by Cait London
In October:	*THE TEXAS BLUE NORTHER* by Lass Small
In November:	*STRYKER'S WIFE* by Dixie Browning
In December:	*CHRISTMAS PAST* by Joan Hohl

**MAN OF THE MONTH...ONLY FROM
SILHOUETTE DESIRE**

MOM96JD

SILHOUETTE DESIRE® "CELEBRATION 1000" SWEEPSTAKES
OFFICIAL RULES—NO PURCHASE NECESSARY

To enter, complete an Official Entry Form or a 3"x5" card by hand printing "Silhouette Desire Celebration 1000 Sweepstakes," your name and address, and mail it to: In the U.S.: Silhouette Desire Celebration 1000 Sweepstakes, P.O. Box 9069, Buffalo, NY 14269-9069, or In Canada: Silhouette Desire Celebration 1000 Sweepstakes, P.O. Box 637, Fort Erie, Ontario L2A 5X3. Limit one entry per envelope. Entries must be sent via first-class mail and be received no later than 6/30/96. No liability is assumed for lost, late or misdirected mail.

Prizes: Grand Prize—an original painting (approximate value $1500 U.S.);300 Runner-up Prizes—an autographed Silhouette Desire® Book (approximate value $3.50 U.S./$3.99 CAN. each). Winners will be selected in a random drawing (to be conducted no later than 9/30/96) from among all eligible entries received by D.L. Blair, Inc., an independent judging organization whose decision is final.

Sweepstakes offer is open only to residents of the U.S. (except Puerto Rico) and Canada who are 18 years of age or older, except employees and immediate family members of Harlequin Enterprises Ltd., their affiliates, subsidiaries, and all agencies, entities and persons connected with the use, marketing or conduct of this sweepstakes. All federal, state, provincial, municipal and local laws apply. Offer void where prohibited by law. Taxes and/or duties are the sole responsibility of the winners. Any litigation within the province of Quebec respecting the conduct and awarding of prizes may be submitted to the Regie des alcools des courses et des jeux. All prizes will be awarded; winners will be notified by mail. No substitution for prizes is permitted. Odds of winning are dependent upon the number of eligible entries received.

Grand Prize winner must sign and return an Affidavit of Eligibility within 30 days of notification. In the event of noncompliance within this time period, prize may be awarded to an alternate winner. Any prize or prize notification returned as undeliverable may result in the awarding of that prize to an alternate winner. By acceptance of their prize, winners consent to the use of their names, photographs or likenesses for purposes of advertising, trade and promotion on behalf of Harlequin Enterprises Ltd., without further compensation unless prohibited by law. In order to win a prize, residents of Canada will be required to correctly answer a time-limited arithmetical skill-testing question administered by mail.

For a list of winners (available after October 31, 1996) send a separate self-addressed stamped envelope to: Silhouette Desire Celebration 1000 Sweepstakes Winners, P.O. Box 4200, Blair, NE 68009-4200.

SWEEPR

SILHOUETTE® *Desire* CELEBRATION 1000

A treasured piece of romance could be yours!

During April, May and June as part of Desire's Celebration 1000 you can enter to win an original piece of art used on an actual Desire cover!

Or you could win one of 300 autographed Man of the Month books!

See Official Sweepstakes Rules for more details.

**The wedding celebration was so nice...
too bad the bride wasn't there!**

Runaway Brides

Find out what happens when three brides have a
change of heart.

Three complete stories by some of your favorite
authors—all in one special collection!

YESTERDAY ONCE MORE
by Debbie Macomber

FULL CIRCLE
by Paula Detmer Riggs

THAT'S WHAT FRIENDS ARE FOR
by Annette Broadrick

Available this June wherever books are sold.

SREQ696

SILHOUETTE... Where Passion Lives

Add these Silhouette favorites to your collection today!
Now you can receive a discount by ordering two or more titles!